THE SPACES IN BETWEEN

A NOVELLA

GAVIN OUGH

SEREALITIES PRESS

WWW.SEREALITIES.COM

ISBN: 0615987737
ISBN-13: 9780615987736
Library of Congress Control Number: 2014904986
Serealities Press, Birmingham, AL

DEDICATION

I would like to dedicate this novelette to my wonderful wife, Kerri, whose belief in and encouragement of me have been instrumental in the writing of this book.

Acknowledgments

Numerous people have to be thanked for their assistance and hard work during the production of my first novelette. For constant support and belief in a talent I didn't think I had, thanks must go the Serealities team, in particular I want to thank Linda and Ed Casebeer. Linda for being in charge of the site and Ed for telling me I had come up with an original idea in this age of remakes and prequels. Massive thanks also go to Anna Carillo without whose dedication, this project would never exist. (Cheers, Anna.) My editor Angela from CreateSpace, for bringing the words to life and correcting all my schoolboy mistakes. Gratitude must also go to the creative team at CreateSpace for the cover art.

Finally, a heartfelt thanks need to go to my children Kenisha, Paige and Marley for putting up with me being a grump when I can't get things to sound right.

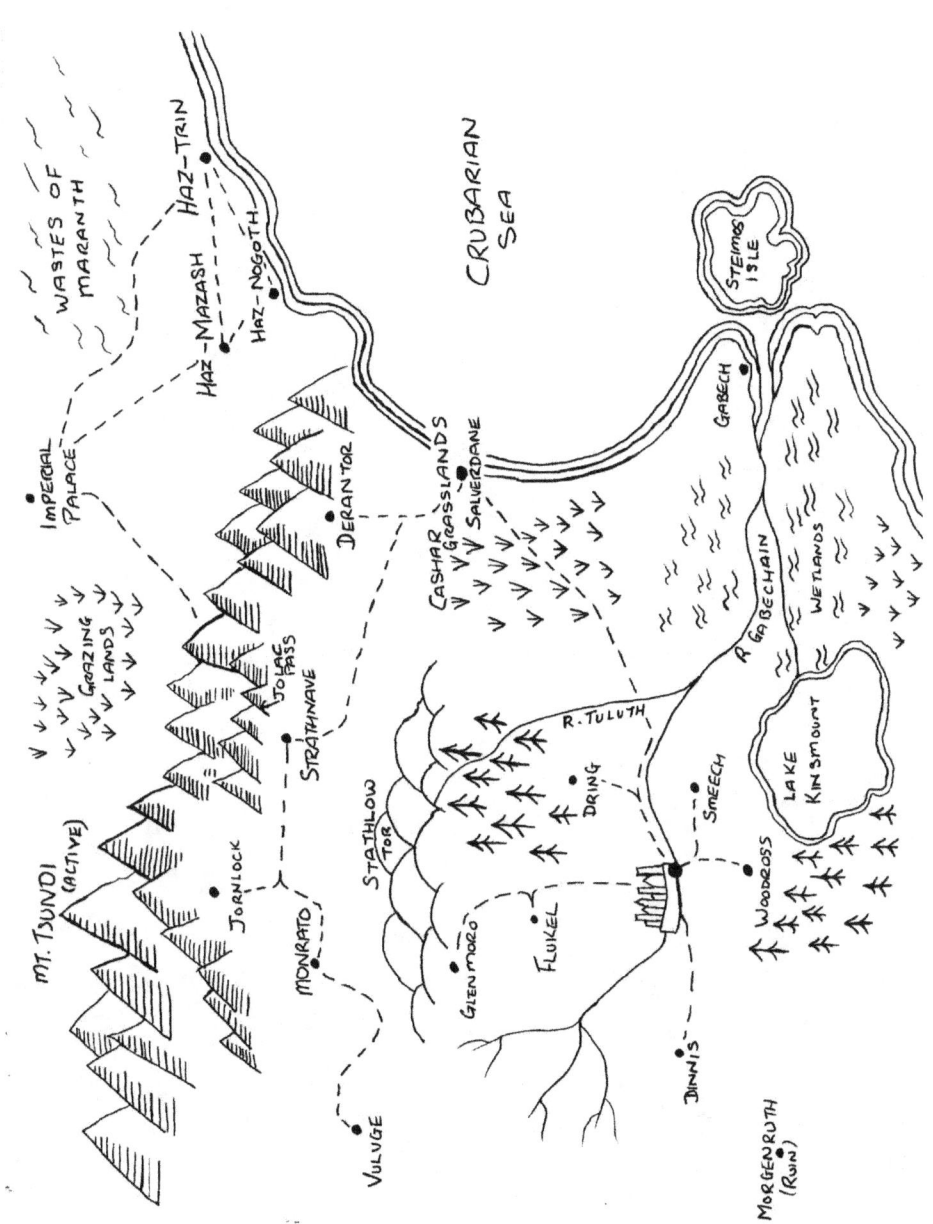

CHAPTER 1

Motes of dust fell lazily, like golden mist, as the toddler silently watched his father cutting and shaping wood with the ease of a seasoned craftsman. The little boy sat—he almost had the patience of a saint—as he daydreamed of the wood nymphs that descended to collect the sawdust each night, using it to help the trees in the forests grow. In his mind's eye, the young Gremlaw actually could see the small creatures collecting the sawdust, their multi-hued wings glinting in the waning sun of the summer afternoon. To the child, daydreaming in his father's small workshop, the nymphs were plainly evident, dancing and cavorting as they filled small sacks with shavings and swept piles of dust with their fluttering wings. Gremlaw looked up to where his father was putting the finishing touches on the table leg he was crafting. The boy studied his father's face; the concentration transformed his features from the careworn ones he ordinarily wore to an almost serene, youthful expression. Gremlaw saw the enjoyment, the sheer pleasure, as his father worked the golden wood, transforming it from a shapeless piece of lumber into a work of art. The toddler beamed, proudly displaying his three new teeth, as the older man looked kindly down at him.

"Shall we go and find your mother?" he asked, reaching down to gently take the small boy's hand.

"Mama!" Gremlaw squealed with youthful exuberance.

Tiny fingers clasped the calloused, larger hand of the parent, and the mismatched pair made its way from the workshop Gremlaw's father had struggled to annex to their home. In the poor trading suburb of Palandine, the capital city of the kingdom of Trathlain, Gremlaw and his father walked into the main area of their home. Cheaply built and meanly furnished, the house was little more than one large room.

Situated on the ground floor, this one room was used for cooking, eating, sleeping, and for any toilet needs, as it had a slop bucket beneath a table. The additional dwelling above the first floor housed two brothers who somehow managed to forage enough income to pay their rent and fund their respective terminal drinking habits. Gremlaw's father made repairs and improvements when he had the time and could scavenge enough materials, yet the conditions remained basic.

Despite the poor living standards, which affected many of the local families, Gremlaw was loved. His parents showered the boy with affection every moment they spent together.

"Where has my little soldier been?" Gremlaw's mother, Cyrena, asked as the pair entered.

On sturdy legs, the young Gremlaw trotted across to his mother, who hoisted him into the air and planted kisses all over his giggling face. Whooping with joy, the youngster pretended to fend off his mother's kisses, running away as she put him back on the floor.

"Your hands look sore, love," his father observed, looking at the red, raw skin covering his wife's fingers and then engulfing her in a hug. Gremlaw's mother worked in a local business washing and dying cloth, and it was the chemicals from this that burned away the flesh from her hands.

"No more than usual," Cyrena said, resting her head on his chest. He knew she was lying as she spoke. "How is it coming along?" She was asking about the table he was building, the sale of which would represent a considerable income boost for the family.

Gremlaw's father smiled at his wife. "Almost finished, love," he told her encouragingly. "I have all the legs finished, and I just need to assemble it." His arms tightened around her. "I'm sorry," he said, his voice thick with emotion. "I never wanted this kind of life for you."

She winced as he took her stinging hands and gently kissed the swollen fingers. "Silly fool," she chided him gently, squeezing his fingers, "if I have you and Gremlaw, this is the best kind of life for me."

The young boy looked up at the mention of his name and, seeing his parents hugging, ran to them. "Me hug too! Me hug too!" he piped in his tiny voice.

Life continued in this way, and as the seasons passed, Gremlaw grew. As an eight-year-old, he occasionally helped his father in his small workshop or assisted his mother in repairing clothing or sweeping their room, and he was happy to do so. His father had managed to get a job building homes in an area that had been ravaged by fire. It was very different from the cabinetry work and fine craftsmanship he enjoyed. The job was difficult and dirty, and the reconstruction sites were notoriously dangerous places, yet Gremlaw's father had insisted it would bring in a substantial sum of money along with a regular wage for the duration of the project.

Three weeks into the building project, tragedy struck. A large load of stone blocks, suspended poorly in a net, broke free of the ropes that held them and smashed the life from Gremlaw's father and two of his coworkers.

Icy fingers of fear clamped tightly around Gremlaw's chest as the stranger delivered this horrific news, standing in his mother's doorway. The young boy's anxiety increased as Cyrena slowly collapsed to the floor after shutting the door. In his youthful, awkward way, he attempted to comfort her by laying a hand upon her shoulder. He felt no movement from her; no sobbing shook her frame. Fear shot through him again as he wondered whether she was even breathing. The youth jumped as his prone mother took in a deep, ragged breath and let out a keening wail of pure loss and anguish for her husband. Gremlaw wrapped his arms around her and cried into her hair; they stayed that way for what seemed like hours.

Eventually Cyrena rose and, with a tear-streaked, devastated face, made sure Gremlaw had access to food before she wordlessly climbed into her solitary bed. The eight-year-old had no idea how to deal with the conflicting emotions he felt as he watched his remaining parent abandon him. Gremlaw wondered whether this somehow had been his fault. Did his mother blame *him* for some reason he was unable to understand? She had made no attempt to comfort him as she wept, even though *he* had tried to hold *her*. Afterward she had not even looked him in the eye; she'd just left her young son alone.

Guilt crashed through his young body and mind like a wave, leaving nothing but feelings of self-loathing as the flood receded. A hollow emptiness grew inside him as he sat heavily upon a chair crafted by his dead father. He folded his arms on the table, placed his head on them, and wept for his loss.

During the next few years, Gremlaw came to know how hard life could become for the poor with virtually no income. His mother had closed herself off from the world, including him. She rose, ate whatever her hand touched first, and left wordlessly for work, like an automaton. Each night Gremlaw lay on his small cot and listened to his mother cry herself to sleep. He made only one more attempt to comfort her as she wept, and while she did not push him away, she did not hug him back. Clueless as to what he had done wrong and hurting so badly that it made breathing difficult, he left her alone. Any help they received from friends and family eventually ceased, leaving a grieving mother and her son to their own devices.

Gremlaw recalled the incident when he realized his mother had begun to lose her sanity. The adolescent had taken up his father's unused tools, trying to craft something from scraps of firewood in the hope he could earn a little money for them. Upon her return from work, Cyrena had stopped and glared at him, causing the smile to fall from his face. Her face transformed from the slack, depressed, haggard visage into a mask of boiling rage. Then she grabbed him by his upper arms and brought his face a hairbreadth of her own.

"Never touch those tools again!" she hissed into his startled face as she shook him violently. The loving mother he once had known was a world away from this woman who squeezed his flesh and shook him in her unfeeling fingers. She dragged Gremlaw away from his father's things and threw him to the floor. "Do you want to end up like him?" she almost screamed. "Well, do you? Dead and gone like he is?" Once again, Gremlaw had no real idea what he done to incite so much rage in the mother who once had loved him, and he rose to his feet, fists clenched in muted anger, fear, and sadness. Not knowing what to say to her, he spun on one heel and sprinted across their single room, slamming the door behind him.

Gremlaw didn't know where he was running to; he just knew he needed to get away from the thing his mother had become. He was trying to run from his pain, trying desperately to run from the searing ache that ate at the heart of his soul. Although tears blurred his vision, the boy wended his way through the crowded streets without crashing into anyone. He didn't stop running until his legs ached and his chest felt as if it would burst. Leaning against a rough wall at the corner of an unknown street, he doubled over and panted, attempting to regain his breath as he scanned the area he found himself in.

Hundreds of stalls were crowded together and peopled by traders from many different cities, countries, and continents. Each stall holder announced loudly that his produce or wares were the best possible quality at the lowest price around, sometimes even shouting about the poorer quality of a neighboring stall's goods. *This must be Catrinse Square*, the boy thought. The square had been the site of a daily market since time immemorial. His father had told him of the almost infinite diversity of this place, but Gremlaw never had been here in person. The sights, sounds, and scents made the boy's mouth drop.

People from races unknown to Gremlaw, of many ages and both genders, mingled and added to the exotic mixture. Groups and individuals alike trawled the stalls, seeking the best bargains available while catching up on the latest news and gossip. Brightly garbed silk traders stood alongside salesmen hawking earthenware, all vying for the coins of passersby. Screaming children sat on the hips of mothers, some in slings in front of or behind them. Groups of men, some armed, made their way along the rows of stalls, seeking specific items of origins unknowable to Gremlaw. In such close quarters and with so many tempting targets, thieves must have been in operation.

Gremlaw knew about thieves from his parents, who had instilled in him a sense of right and wrong; his father had taught him that stealing was against the law, and people who stole were the target of the local watch. While the youth knew about criminals, he never had met or even seen one, as far as he knew, and his mind created monstrous images of dark-clad figures with red, glowing eyes armed to the teeth with swords and daggers—men who randomly would slay anyone of their choosing for a few copper coins. In reality, the first crime he actually witnessed was committed by a girl who appeared younger than he was.

The little girl caught his eye as he studied the masses of people passing one another, creating patterns like eddies in a stream. Gremlaw's youthful, untrained eye became aware of spaces in between and areas around the slowly moving crush of people. Almost as if in a rehearsed dance, everyone seemed to acknowledge these areas and abide by a set of unwritten and probably subconscious rules; as the boy looked harder, he noticed these spaces were maintained automatically. Even people who had their backs to one another seemingly were able to sense their proximity and reposition themselves accordingly so they were not too close. As Gremlaw watched in fascination, his attention was caught by a small figure who did not seem to pay any attention to the unspoken rules. Being smaller than almost everyone else, the girl commanded no attention whatsoever from anyone else.

Long, almost white-blond hair framed a small, serious-looking face; her green eyes darted everywhere, capturing any and all details of her surroundings. Her ragged, filthy clothes barely concealed her tiny, thin frame, although she did seem lucid and alert. As Gremlaw watched her, transfixed, she approached one of the stalls that carried breads and other baked goods. She scanned the area for any dangers and, deeming all was safe, casually reached up and claimed a small loaf. A sudden cold fear welled up in Gremlaw's chest as he witnessed the theft. What would happen if she were caught? Would the watch imprison a child? Would he be taken as well for having seen it and not reported it? His mind raced as possibilities and scenarios flashed through his consciousness. In actuality, however, the small girl simply walked slowly away from the stall she had just robbed and lost herself in the gaps and spaces between the crowds.

Gremlaw followed her progress as she made her way closer to where he stood, pulling morsels away from the loaf and stuffing them hungrily into her small mouth. Abruptly she looked up from her meal and directly into his eyes. A shock of something close to recognition flowed through Gremlaw even though he never had seen her before. Her sparkling emerald eyes held his gaze as she considered him, almost analytically, for approximately three seconds, before awarding the boy with the most dazzling, beautiful smile he ever had received. He stood, transfixed again, as she approached him and offered him a large chunk of bread.

"Want some?" she asked in a high-pitched, clear voice.

Gremlaw extended a trembling hand and took the offered bread; he was definitely in trouble now that he had stolen bread in his hand. A small voice he never had heard before, however, casually told him if he ate the bread, there would be no way for the watch to prove he'd had it. Hunger coursed through him as the fresh bread awoke his baser senses.

The little girl smiled beautifully again as he devoured the remaining food.

"My name's Huleta," she informed him. "What's yours?"

"Gremlaw," he managed to utter around a mouthful of bread.

"Gremlaw," she repeated slowly, as if speaking the word were difficult. "You ain't one of us, is you?" she added quizzically.

Gremlaw was puzzled. "One of you?"

"Yes," she replied sweetly. "A street runner, like me."

The boy shook his head. "No." His tone was almost apologetic. "How can you tell?"

Huleta grinned, grabbed his hand, and waved it before his eyes. "You're too clean to be living in streets," she told him. "And your clothes ain't got no holes in them!" She let his hand drop but kept hold of it, which warmed Gremlaw's entire body.

"Have you ever been caught?" Gremlaw wondered.

It appeared Huleta was aware he had witnessed her crime, but she did not seem bothered by it in the least. "Never," she declared with a hint of pride. "The watch is too fixed on the older ones to notice me. And anyway I go in the gaps, what's in between people." The girl straightened from the wall she had been leaning against and added in a not unfriendly tone, "Well, Gremlaw, I hope to see you round sometime." With that, she planted a firm kiss on the startled boy's lips, released his hand, and darted into the crowd.

Gremlaw made his slow way home in a daze with a silly smile across his face. He did not even mind as a group of older boys teased him for being simple as he walked; he merely placed one foot in front of the other while attempting to recall every aspect of his first kiss.

His mother snatched the door open as she heard him begin to open it, and he flinched, fearing a repeat of the earlier outburst as she swooped down toward him. Her intentions this time, however, were completely different, and she caught him in a tight embrace, pulling his head to her shoulder and cradling him there. Through her sobbing, he could just make out her repeated words—"I'm so sorry"—as she rocked him from side to side. Sensing this was something she needed to experience, and enjoying the sensations of being held once more, Gremlaw remained still and quiet. His mother led him inside and stationed herself upon a chair, leaning him back to look into his face with an expression of disgust on her own. "I never should have laid hands on you like that," she said. "I have no idea what came over me, but when I saw you standing at your father's bench with his tools..." She trailed off.

"You thought I would end up like him?" Gremlaw asked in a small voice. Cyrena nodded as her face collapsed into tears once more. "I just thought I might be able to help make us some money, Mama," he told her as his lip trembled. "I don't understand what I did wrong."

"Nothing, my beautiful boy," she said as she held him tightly. "You did nothing wrong. It was all my fault. *This* is all my fault."

Later, after they had eaten a small supper and cleared the dishes away, they lay in his mother's bed, facing each other. They talked late into the night about his father, and she told him how they had met. Gremlaw had heard the tales many times before yet relished every word as his mother's voice soothed the heartache he had felt earlier.

More and more often, Gremlaw found himself in Catrinse Square. He told himself he went there to study the patterns of people and the spaces that flowed between and around them, training his eyes to look for what was not there rather than what was. Of course, the possibility that he might have a second chance encounter with the enigmatic Huleta was never far from his mind. As time passed, Gremlaw realized he might have to take some kind of action soon. His mother had sold his father's tools for a pittance to pay for food and clothing for the growing boy. While never returning to her previous distant state, she became even more quiet and withdrawn, sometimes only complaining about their lack of money and the scarcity of work.

Gremlaw spent a great deal of time in thought as he stood on the periphery of the marketplace, considering numerous points mainly concerning the watch and their ignorance toward what he now termed "negative space." Although Gremlaw had led a sheltered life with his parents, he certainly was not stupid or naïve in any way. The thought came to him that if he and Huleta were aware of the negative spaces, others also would be able to see them, which naturally would encompass some of the members of the Watch. Briefly, Gremlaw considered joining the ranks of the watch and assisting in the capture of thieves, yet he dismissed the idea almost immediately, as he did not relish the years of training involved in joining the watch.

The boy had spent too many days going hungry and decided today would be the day he began to take responsibility for himself. Gremlaw spent more than an hour opposite the stall he had decided upon, studying the actions of the vendor, the circulation of the watch, and the position of any customers as they shopped or passed by. He chose a particularly busy time for the stall, just as a fresh tray of roasted meats was delivered; the aroma of the cooking drew a large crowd, and Gremlaw knew this was the time. Heart in mouth and with growing apprehension, he slowly approached the side edge of the stall. The seller was rushing from one end to the other in an attempt to provide food to the throng of milling customers and took no interest in the grubby-faced boy who hovered at the edge of the crowd. Gremlaw spied a piece of meat on a slab of bread that was left over from the tray of meats on sale earlier. Almost casually, he reached out as the seller stood at the opposite end of the stall and, with a trembling hand, plucked the meat-laden bread from its resting place. Fear building inside him, Gremlaw strolled away as calmly as he was able. With each step he took, a feeling of elation built; as he sampled the bread base of the meal he had stolen, a stab of guilt shot through him. Although it was cold and grease had begun to congeal on the bread, the meat tasted more delicious than anything he had eaten in recent months.

"Stop, thief!"

Gremlaw's stomach fell as he heard the shout from behind him. He froze, with meat juice running down his face, and his hand halfway to his mouth once more, as the sound of feet approached his position. All the feelings of elation and even the guilt dissolved in that moment to be replaced by a deep fear of what was to come. Would he be imprisoned? Hanged? Gremlaw decided if he were to die for this crime, he would at least finish the food he had snatched. Stuffing great mouthfuls of the bread and meat into his mouth, he barely chewed, swallowing the food as fast as he could.

His mouth went completely dry as a violent trembling set into his body and a small hand clapped his shoulder. "Ain't you got no more to share?" the clear, sweet voice of Huleta asked as Gremlaw jumped at her touch. "What's wrong with y..." The girl trailed off as she noticed he was about to pass out, be sick, cry, or all three. "You didn't think...?" Huleta stopped as she began to laugh. The pained expression on Gremlaw's face made her chuckle all the more. "The look on your face!" Her shoulders shook as she nearly collapsed in helpless gales of laughter.

Gremlaw felt a mixture of relief at not being caught by the watch, stupidity for having thought Huleta's voice was that of a man, and anger at her for playing this trick on him. Her pure peals of laughter drove him over the edge into outright rage, and he shouted into her tear-lined face, "It's not funny!"

Huleta doubled over, reaching out for him to steady herself as breathing started to get complicated. Soon Gremlaw found her laughter more than a little infectious, and combined with his relief at not being caught, he found himself joining her in mirth. Eventually the pair calmed a little and managed to stand. Huleta had her hand on her aching stomach muscles and broke out into a fit of giggles at the slightest look from Gremlaw.

"I thought I'd be hanged," Gremlaw stated with a straight face, which brought another round of laughter, interspersed with moans of pain.

"Stop!" Huleta whined. "It hurts!"

"Good!" the offended youth retorted unkindly. "It should hurt."

Huleta looked at him to see if he was joking and noticed the smile on his face. As her giggling subsided, the pair made a slow walk from the marketplace, emerging into an area of the city with which Gremlaw was unfamiliar.

Apparently, no one in this area was responsible for clearing the waste and detritus from the streets, as rotting excrement, food scraps, and worse were piled against the bases of the buildings. His face a mask of disgust, Gremlaw almost retched at the vile odor of the place. Disrepair and decay seemed to affect all the buildings here, and he felt as if the narrow streets were closing in on them, claustrophobia making his imagination run wild.

"You get used to the smell," Huleta stated quietly. "Eventually," she added solemnly.

"Why are we even here?" Gremlaw asked as she led him into an alley between two wooden structures so old they had fallen against each other overhead.

Through the gloom and dirt, Huleta guided him until they reached what looked to be a dead end. She looked up into Gremlaw's eyes for a second before snatching her gaze away. "We're here 'cos this is where I live," she uttered in a tiny voice before pulling aside a collection of rotting planks that appeared to be held together by strips of canvas. Huleta crouched and disappeared into the black maw she had uncovered.

Several notions struck Gremlaw simultaneously; Huleta had wanted to bring him here, to her home, for some reason. His reaction of disgust and revulsion had upset and embarrassed the girl, and he felt guilty for this. It was one of the first times he was able to recall empathizing with someone else, and even more guilt hit him as he thought about how he should have been able to experience this kind of feeling for his mother. As new feelings vied for Gremlaw's attention, he took a deep breath and climbed through the hole.

In a nest of scavenged rags and blankets, Huleta sat hugging her scabbed knees. Her "home" appeared to be a hole underneath the buildings they had been walking past; Gremlaw saw joists and floorboards above his head. Three of the walls that formed the boundaries of her home were massive stone blocks; the fourth, the one they had crawled through to get in, was wooden. With the dim light afforded through the mean entrance, Gremlaw made out a few items Huleta had collected: a pair of cracked earthenware cups, one with the handle snapped off; a carved wooden horse with only three legs; and a string of cheaply made beads that hung on a rusty nail jutting dangerously from one wall. Beside her, in what he assumed was her bed, Huleta had a vaguely human-shaped bundle of rags that Gremlaw eventually recognized as a doll. This apparently was the sum total of the girl's possessions, and it made his heart ache to see his friend looking so despondent at introducing him to her home.

Although the area was cramped, it was dry, and even the stench from outside was unable to penetrate within. He smelled an old musty odor combined with just a hint of Huleta's personal scent.

"This is cozy," Gremlaw said with a smile.

Her head snapped up to see whether he was making fun, but he had made the comment genuinely, and she smiled back, making his innards squirm for some reason he could not understand. Gremlaw crawled in the rest of the way and curled himself around the edge of her sleeping area with his back to one of the stone blocks.

"It ain't much," she whispered, "but it's somewhere dry to sleep."

"How long have you lived here?" Gremlaw wondered as he shifted position to make himself more comfortable. He yawned, as the last traces of his earlier adrenaline rush had long left his system and tiredness had kicked in.

"Just a couple of years," Huleta said, stretching herself out and facing him.

He gazed into her emerald eyes as he asked his next question, surmising the answer before he did so. Staring straight into her eyes, he asked, "Where are your parents?" He noticed them change; saw the hardness that framed them.

Huleta took a deep breath before she answered him. "My da got killed at sea when his ship got sinked," she said with a bleakness that cut Gremlaw deeply and brought back his own loss. "My ma had to…She started…entertaining?" Huleta left her sentence in a question, hoping Gremlaw would understand. Looking at his puzzled face, she added, "Men. Entertaining men." Gremlaw eventually got a vague idea of what she was referring to and just nodded, not passing any kind of judgment. Huleta was quiet for a few seconds then continued. "One night I heard my ma screaming and a man shouting. Then there was this big crash, and it all went quiet." Her voice hitched on the last word, and Gremlaw suddenly had no desire to hear what had happened next.

Tears made her lovely eyes shimmer as she continued with her story. "I waited until I heard him go away then went to see if Ma was all right." Huleta tried to swallow her pain with a large gulp. "When I went into the bit where she slept, she was…was…" Gremlaw reached out and pulled her against his chest as she broke down in tears, her tiny form racked with sobs. Eventually she managed to calm herself down. "I didn't know there was so much blood inside someone," she whispered, "not until I saw the puddle what had come out of my ma."

Gremlaw's throat was so tightly closed that he could not have said anything even if he had known what to say. He felt a primal need to protect this young girl, an urge he had no idea how to carry out, as she was probably more capable of looking after herself than he was. He vowed to himself that he would do anything and everything he could to make her life better. Tentatively he stroked her silken hair, which elicited a sound of satisfied appreciation from her.

CHAPTER 2

Since that day, Gremlaw and Huleta were nearly inseparable. They played together, stole together, and grew up together, always reliant on each other, as they had no one else. Gremlaw's mother became ever more distant as the years passed, and she became a virtual stranger to him, lost inside her own mind. Once she no longer could work, Gremlaw, through his exploits, took care of her as best he could, providing food and even managing to pay their rent.

The young man rose each day and prepared some kind of meal for his mother, made sure she had eaten, and settled her in a comfortable chair with a ragdoll Huleta had fashioned for her. Once, his mother had gripped his upper arm as he eased her into the chair, and in a moment of absolute clarity, she said, "I love you, Son, and I'm proud of you." Gremlaw was shocked yet pleased, as most of the time she barely registered his presence, often calling him "Rhican," his father's name.

"I love you too, Ma," he said, smiling, but his mother already had retreated into herself.

Once he was sure his mother was safe, he would exit his home and climb the stairs, knocking on the door that Huleta would answer. She had come by the little home above Gremlaw's when he noticed a foul smell coming from upstairs and had gone up to discover the Adwarin brothers had choked each other to death, seemingly over a bottle. It had taken a couple of days of summer heat for the odor of putrefaction to reach his nostrils, but once it had, he had called the watch and the land-lord, the latter of whom seemed more concerned with his loss of income than the two dead men, until Gremlaw suggested he knew someone who might want the place. Knowing two men had killed each other in the room, Huleta was a little apprehensive at first, until Gremlaw revealed it was the room above his own and had been thoroughly scrubbed clean.

Although small in stature, Gremlaw had grown up strong, wiry, lithe, acrobatic, and fast. He and Huleta had chased each other through the streets and parks of the city, childish games that had turned them both into athletes. It was during these games that Gremlaw uncovered some of his ability to see the negative spaces in between people and objects, and he frequently used these as a means of escape after a theft.

Recently he and Huleta had been quite happily sitting in one of the public parks, enjoying the sunshine and each other's company. Their bellies were full due to the successful robbery of one of the new eating-houses that had sprung up in Palandine. The pair had worked out a quick plan before walking into the establishment and weaving them-selves between the tables. Due to the early hour, the place was empty, and they headed to the rear of the premises before being challenged.

"Help you?" a surly, ruddy-faced man demanded with a scowl. He held a long knife in one hand as he came from the kitchen.

"It's my sister," Gremlaw growled in mock exasperation as Huleta looked at the floor as if ashamed. "She needs a job," he added, rolling his eyes. The cook or owner—Gremlaw did not care which—looked Huleta up and down appreciatively, noticing her body and probably thinking he would be able to take advantage of her once she worked there.

"Let's talk," the knife-holding man said, indicating a chair.

With a subtlety born of practice, Gremlaw managed to steer the man to sit with his back to Huleta and began the entirely fictitious haggling process. The young woman slipped into the kitchen area unseen and proceeded to rifle through the produce they had seen delivered half an hour earlier.

Gremlaw kept the man haggling over money and hours for at least five minutes until he turned around to have another look at the girl he was about to hire. He stood quickly, an expression of distrust and anger on his face. "Where did she go?" he demanded.

Gremlaw made a little circular gesture next to his temple. "She wanders," he said, shrugging as the man darted for the kitchen. Gremlaw waited a few seconds before making his way calmly from the open-fronted establishment and disappearing into the throng of people milling around outside. Huleta joined him at the place they had agreed to meet, after taking a circuitous route away from the back door of the restaurant with their meal.

The pair ate, Gremlaw making sure he took some home for his mother, and they even drifted off into sleep, side by side on the grass, until clouds the color of slate announced the arrival of a summer storm.

"Race you back?" Huleta suggested, glancing at the storm.

Gremlaw kept a completely straight face as he replied, "Not much of a challenge."

Huleta punched him playfully on the arm and stood, stretching her lithe form, which Gremlaw never tired of looking at.

"Come on," she said. "I ain't going to get caught out in that." She gestured to the sky with her chin. "I'll make it easy on you—you know, what with you being older than me and all." They had worked out that Gremlaw was approximately eighteen months older than Huleta, and she teased him playfully about it at every opportunity.

"Just let me get my cane, and help an old man to his feet," Gremlaw joked along with her, making his voice sound like that of a weak, elderly man. "Then I'll teach you some respect, you young whippersnapper!" Huleta giggled; she loved it when he performed some imitation or mimicked the voices he heard around the city.

Gremlaw sprung to his feet and bounced on his toes, rolling his shoulders and making sure the food he carried was secure. He glanced at Huleta and grinned.

"One," he said.

"Two," she added.

"Three!" they shouted at the same time, springing into action and racing across the grass.

Gremlaw had the slightest edge, as he could accelerate faster, but Huleta's longer legs allowed her to catch up to him over longer distances, and as they reached the perimeter wall of the public park, they ran side by side. Gremlaw launched himself through the gateway, skidding a little as his foot came down on the cobbled street. Huleta threw out her hand, her long fingers catching the smooth stone of the wall, which she used as leverage to orient herself toward the area where they both lived.

Something odd seemed to happen to Gremlaw's eyesight as he loped along the paved streets, dodging around people and even vaulting over a low handcart being pulled by an old woman. The old woman shook her fist at the grinning youth and called him some choice names, even though he made the jump without touching the items she had collected. Gremlaw shook his head as he ran, trying to make his vision clear and to return to normal. His eyes told him the world had transformed, highlighting the spaces that existed between and around things. Abruptly he realized he could see negative space more clearly than whatever framed it. A strange sense of elation filled him as he raced for each gap, which appeared as a basic shape surrounded by a feathery green outline. Gremlaw looked off farther into the distance and noticed some of the green-lined areas seemed to line up, indicating a pathway of unobstructed, open running space. Heads turned and men pointed as they saw the laughing youth tear between them in what seemed to be a reckless way.

Gremlaw ran as fast as he could through city streets crowded with people, beasts of burden, and the various objects they had with them. His new mode of vision allowed him to avoid everything in his path. At one point he had a surprise, as a heavily laden wagon shifted in front of him, but he threw himself forward and rolled beneath the deck, coming to his feet and sprinting toward his home.

Huleta almost made it home before the storm. She was two streets away when the storm clouds that had threatened to pour their contents over the city did in fact pour their contents over the city. Within ten heartbeats, she was soaked to the skin. Her light blond hair was plastered to her neck, and her clothing stuck to her uncomfortably. Women squealed as the deluge hammered the crowds, making passage virtually impossible as people scattered left and right. The only thought that made Huleta even slightly happy was that Gremlaw would be suffering the same fate. Finally reaching the narrow stone steps that led to her door, she felt elated, as Gremlaw was nowhere to be seen. If he had gone in to see his mother, he would have left the door open for Huleta, especially in this rain.

Huleta pulled a large key from beneath her clothing and slammed it home into the simple lock that held her door closed. She turned the key and slipped inside, slamming the door shut and locking it. She leaned her soaking forehead against the rough wooden planks as she tried to regain her breath. Huleta almost screamed when she heard his voice.

"Damp out, is it?"

She spun on one heel. "Gremlaw!" the young woman cried, her eyes wide with fright. "You nearly scared the life out of me!" She noticed his clothing was dry as he leaned against the wall. "How did you...? How long have you...?" Gremlaw's gray eyes were fixed on her, a smoldering expression on his face. Huleta never had seen this look on his face before, and it made odd things clench inside her stomach. Almost as if she were unable to resist, she took an involuntary step toward her guest. Gremlaw's eyes seemed to flash in the dimness of the room as he slowly took a few steps toward her.

Gremlaw gently pushed Huleta against the rough wood of the door, pressing his lips against hers and gripping her soft neck. Huleta was aware of his lean, hard body pressed against her own before she gave in to the kiss and brought her arms up to grip the back of his head, hands fisting in his hair. When Gremlaw finally broke their kiss, Huleta remained in the same position, eyes closed and lips pouting as if they still felt his lips upon them. She exhaled a deep breath she hadn't known she'd been holding and swallowed.

"What was *that*?" she whispered hoarsely.

She felt Gremlaw's body move as he laughed gently. "A kiss?" His deep voice reverberated through her chest as she opened her eyes.

Gazing into Gremlaw's own stare, his face so near they shared breath, Huleta felt a surge of desire burn within her body, heating her face and stomach as her pulse quickened. She leaned forward and took his bottom lip between her own, feeling him, tasting him. Huleta never had experienced anything like this before; in fact, she had unconsciously avoided men because of what had happened…to her mother.

Huleta shoved Gremlaw away, nearly falling as she did. "No!" she shouted. "No! I…I can't!" Immediately hurt by the look of pained confusion on his face yet unable to comprehend what to do, Huleta crossed her arms and refused to meet his stare. "I'm sorry, Grem," she said quietly as she moved aside, "but I think you should go."

"Do you want to talk about this?" Gremlaw asked in a controlled voice.

"Just go," she answered flatly.

Gremlaw took a deep breath, which Huleta was sure would signify the beginning of his shouting at her; after all, that was nearly always what had happened to her mother. Next would come the beatings—fists against flesh and screams of pain—as her mother lay on the floor being repeatedly kicked. As Gremlaw opened the wooden door, Huleta felt a sudden stab of panic. "Are we still friends?" she asked in a small voice.

Gremlaw did not turn as he answered, "Of course we are." His voice was steady despite the tears that mingled with the summer rain.

He went in to see his mother, fed her, and made sure of her toilet needs before settling her back in the chair and curling himself up in a pile of blankets on the floor. *What's wrong with me?* He wondered. What was it about him that made everyone he loved leave him? His father had died and left him; his mother had retreated into the realms of her mind and left him; and now the woman he loved, Huleta, had shoved him away and told him to go. Why? What was so inherently evil about him that made people leave? Gremlaw pondered these questions as he lay shivering beneath his rough blankets, wallowing in self-pity. Eventually he fell asleep.

* * *

Gremlaw watched closely from one of his usual vantage points as the large merchant wandered through the market square, his fat purse dangling seductively from a belt at his round waist. He was dressed in the same style as some of the other men who walked the marketplace looking for bargains and trade opportunities, all red velvet with gold trim and cream silk gathered in an attempt to hide the vast circumference of his gut.

The young man had decided to gather as much coin as he could in the next few days and then leave. *As simple as that,* Gremlaw thought. Make a new life someplace where he had no ties. His one regret was leaving his mother and Huleta, but he doubted his departure would affect Huleta too badly, and his mother probably would not even notice. It was better to make a clean break and keep other people at a distance to avoid getting hurt.

He allowed his gaze to take in the wares of the stalls around him, the din of shouting hawkers and screaming children not off-putting at all, as he followed the regally dressed trader through the throng. This merchant had been Gremlaw's target since he had spotted him more than two hours ago. A wily one, this merchant, for sure, he had been wending his way through the market comparing prices from different stalls before returning to the cheapest to purchase his goods. Gremlaw knew he had no guards or porters, no one who could act as witness or alert the watch, relying on his clothing and status as a member of the merchants' guild to protect him. As the youth decided to make his move, ice-cold fingers of nervous anticipation caught hold of his stomach.

Gremlaw walked casually through wide gaps toward the rotund trader, stopping to examine a few cheaply made trinkets at one of the stalls opposite his target.

"You look like you need to own one of the finest handwrought, pure-gold charms this city has to offer, young sir!"

Gremlaw looked at the blackened teeth of the man who was trying to foist rubbish off as finery. He thought about just leaving and getting the purse he had been watching for hours, but the trials of the past couple of days had soured his mood, and he could not resist having a little fun at this shoddily dressed man's expense.

"This?" he exclaimed loudly, pointing to the few dull items the man had for sale. Gremlaw looked at the man with an incredulous expression. "You call *this* the finest in the city?"

The stall holder made calming, placating gestures with his hands. "Of course not, young sir," the rotten-mouthed man said in a pleading tone. "A thousand apologies."

Gremlaw reached for a brooch that was so crudely made it might have been fashioned by a toddler. Hefting it in his hand, he widened his eyes even farther. "This isn't even gold!" he cried loudly. A small crowd was forming now, their interest piqued by the altercation between these two men. "Painted copper! That's what this is!" Gremlaw shouted, having no idea what the metal was, other than it was *not* gold. "Someone ought to call the watch!" he added.

"There will be no need, young sir!" the stall holder squealed, as he eyed the increasingly hostile crowd. "I will be leaving now." Although the shabbily dressed man had laid his wares out on a snatch cloth—ya cloth that simply had a long, thin rope sewn into the hem of the cloth, which when jerked hard, turned it into a sack for carrying anything placed on top—he was not about to escape the crowd of booing men and women who had gathered around him. Gremlaw took the opportunity to slip into an arch-shaped space between two men who had raised their fists in anger.

Making sure the sliver of a blade attached to a ring on his middle finger was positioned correctly, Gremlaw followed behind his quarry, glancing around once more before whipping his hand out as the wealthy merchant's hand pushed the ever emptying purse toward his side. Gremlaw slit the velvet purse and felt coins hit his palm, the cacophony from the market covering the sound of the coins clinking musically against one another.

A familiar surge of elation swept through Gremlaw as he completed the theft, to be replaced by cold fright as his wrist was caught in a hot, sweaty, chubby hand. The merchant had caught him.

"Thief!" screamed the man as Gremlaw struggled vainly to free himself from the impressive grip. He already could see what looked like the watch bulling their way through the crowd to take him to a caged wagon, where he would wait to be dragged off to the nearest gaol. Several of the watchmen "accidentally" punched and kicked him as they dragged him toward a wheeled cage, surrounded by children throwing food and excrement through the bars and hitched to a bored-looking donkey.

"Name?" a burly, black-haired watchman growled from behind a fortress-like desk just beyond the door of the local gaol.

"Elspeth," Gremlaw spat, receiving a hard slap as he gave a woman's name.

Eventually he was hauled to a grimy underground cell with moisture running down the walls and dumped inside. After shouting abuse at the men who had deposited him there and hearing their derisive laughter, Gremlaw settled on the cold floor; somehow, sleep came.

"Get up!" an aristocratic voice commanded sometime later.

Gremlaw's eyes opened as he was unceremoniously dragged to his feet. Before him stood a man who wore the traditional court dress; hosiery covered his legs, and his feet were shod in what appeared to be flimsy slippers. He wore a purple brocaded tunic with small pearls sewn into it with gold-and-silver thread, and around his neck dangled a golden chain from which hung a golden disc the size of Gremlaw's palm; upon its face was inscribed the insignia of the kingdom of Trathlain and the royal coat of arms. His fingers carried a pair of mismatched yet hefty rings, one of which was set with a blood-red ruby the size of a runner bean seed.

"You have two options," the finely dressed man growled, "work for me or stay here and take your punishment."

When Gremlaw smiled grimly and spat on the man's shoes, he received a rough shove back into the cell. Fear, hate, and misery crawled through him as he lay in the mildewy underground cell. If he were in prison, how would his mother fare? It seemed he had no choice but to see what this snooty man wanted.

CHAPTER 3

In the three days that followed, Gremlaw explored every inch of his moldy cell—even down to tossing through the damp straw upon which he had avoided sleeping. One of the smaller stones had begun to come loose from the back wall, and rust plagued the iron hinges that held the substantial door in place. A connection fired inside his head as he thought he might be able to hammer his way through the rusty hinges.

As the youth worked to free the loose stone, he kept his ears tuned for any footfalls from patrolling guards. When he heard none, he was spurred on in his desperate plan to escape. Like a tooth being pulled from a jaw, the fist-size stone came free of the wall and sat in Gremlaw's hand. He immediately crossed to the door and smashed the stone against the rusty hinges in an attempt to loosen it enough to escape. He managed to take off the flakes of rust that coated the exterior of the metal. Then he worked his way through to the cleaner metal beneath, only to find that it was still thick enough to hold the door fast. Desperation crept into Gremlaw as he squatted on the floor. This feeling was followed by anger that threatened to boil over into a rage, which might end up luring him into doing something foolish.

"Hey!" Gremlaw shouted into the darkness beyond. "Guard!"

The tapping of footsteps alerted him to someone's presence, and he stood back from the door, ready to face whoever was on the other side.

"What's with all the banging?" a gruff voice demanded.

Neurons in Gremlaw's brain fired in rapid order, giving him an idea. "I want to talk to the fop who offered me work," he shouted through the wooden door.

Cocky laughter met his words. "DeLarouge said you'd be more agreeable after a few days in here, and don't you be calling him a fop neither. He's Duke Wattiern DeLarouge."

Gremlaw heard the jingling of large keys as the door was unlocked and noticed his vision shift as the wood swung inward. His mind picked out the darker area, outlined in pale green again, which was bordered by the guard's leg and the doorframe. As soon as the portal opened, he darted through the hole that had been created, rolling on his shoulder before sprinting along the grimy corridor beyond.

"Hey!" the guard yelled as Gremlaw disappeared from his view.

Gremlaw ran as fast as he could, his lungs burning with the effort as he climbed a flight of stone stairs into a more brightly lit area. A single guard sat idly beside a door at the end of a corridor lined on both sides with iron bars holding cells closed. The man's expression of shocked surprise would have been comical in other circumstances. As the guard stood to block the door, Gremlaw's vision compensated, outlining the spaces he might be able to fit through and those he could not. Gremlaw sprinted along the corridor, encouraged by the howls and calls he heard from within a few of the cells. The youth dove into the inverted V made by the guard's legs, slid along on his chest and stomach for a few feet, and scrambled up, fumbling the door latch open to bolt out into the sunlight. Two burly guards started to give chase until a bejeweled hand halted their progress.

"Let him go," the authoritative voice of Duke Wattiern DeLarouge stated. "We have a small surprise waiting for him at his home." The duke leaned down from the morose-looking animal he rode and added, "You two would not be able to keep up with him anyway."

Grays and browns blended with reds and greens into a whirl of color as Gremlaw ran like the wind toward home, dodging through the wide spaces people left between them as if by unwritten agreement. Negative spaces lit up in a green-outlined serpentine stretch through the streets. The young man thought the effect might even be beautiful to look at if he ever had the chance to see it while not running headlong toward some goal. Gremlaw skirted around the perimeter of Catrinse Square. Most of the stall holders had packed up for the day, but the watch would still be vigilant, and he had to get home. He had to make plans for his mother's future welfare if he were going to be gone for any length of time. Huleta would help him; he was sure, despite what had happened between them. From the marketplace, Gremlaw skipped along the familiar ways until he reached the street where he was born. Pausing as if to catch his breath, he made sure there were no guards or watchmen waiting for him; he even scanned along the roofs. Twenty-eight steps later, he slipped through his front door.

No sooner had Gremlaw entered the small room than he sensed something was wrong. His mother wore an almost peaceful expression as she rocked the ragdoll, and a younger woman stood next to her. Clad in a simple brown wool dress, the young woman had a plain, round face and straight chestnut hair held back in a simple leather thong.

"Dear brother!" this newcomer exclaimed loudly. "Mother has been expecting you. Wherever have you been?" Gremlaw flinched from the stare his faux sister burned into him and nearly recoiled from the false smile that never came close to including her eyes. His mother had the remains of a meal before her, so at least whoever this was had been feeding her, Gremlaw noticed, as rage built in his chest once more. Who did these people think they were? How was it possible for *royalty* to treat their subjects in this manner? Gremlaw wondered this, as he knew as sure as day turned to night, that this woman had something to do with the duke.

The heat of anger welling in his chest made it feel as if his blood were boiling as he watched this fake sister help *his* mother to her bed. As soon as his "sister" returned to the front of the room, Gremlaw was on her in a blur of action. He grasped her by the throat, his hungry fingers digging into her larynx, and hammered her into the stone wall as she began to redden and choke.

"Who are you, and what have you done to my mother?" he hissed into her shocked face. Gremlaw had both hands around the woman's neck, which made it almost impossible for her to answer. She panicked, raking her fingers down his arms and trying to reach his face. Gremlaw felt the pulse in her neck, her muscles straining for air as her throat worked, and still he kept the pressure on her throat. Her hands began to lose strength, making her attacks less painful, and just as her eyes began to glaze over, Gremlaw let her drop to the floor.

Drawing in a huge lungful of life-giving air, she made an inhuman growling whine of a sound, as if the act of breathing hurt her. Gremlaw looked down with a pitiless expression; he had been badly abused himself in the past few days and felt nothing for this woman who had so easily convinced his mother's broken, damaged mind that she was the daughter she'd never had. The woman made choking sounds as her body fought for life and breath in equal measure.

Showing no pity, Gremlaw kicked her in the leg. "I asked you a question," he reminded her in a harsh tone.

Instead of speaking, she reached into a hidden pocket within her dress and pulled out a small stoppered bottle, sliding it before Gremlaw on the cold stone floor.

Stooping to pick up the quail's-egg-size bottle, Gremlaw asked, "What's this?"

Still choking from the near throttling, the woman hoarsely whispered, "Antidote."

Cold fear ran through Gremlaw at this word, and his anger drained away. "Antidote for what?" he demanded, already knowing the answer.

"The poison that even now courses through your mother's veins." She coughed out the last two words through her bruised throat.

Gremlaw thought for a moment before handing the bottle back to the surprised woman, who had managed to get to her knees. "I suppose you work for DeLarouge?" Her single nod was all the answer he required. "And where do I find the good duke?" he asked sarcastically. Once Gremlaw had a place where he could make contact with DeLarouge, he turned to leave. Reaching the door, he paused with his hand on the latch but turned to look at the woman who was pretending to be the sister he'd never had. She was watching his every move with an almost triumphant smile. Gremlaw jumped toward her, slamming one hand into the wall on either side of her head. The woman let out a squeal and jumped, banging her face into the stone as she tried to turn her head away. Gremlaw saw the pulse jumping madly in her throat as fright crashed into her.

"If I find out you've mistreated my ma in *any* way," Gremlaw snarled into her ear as she cowered, "I'll come back." He copied Huleta's way of speaking as he added, "And if I come back, I ain't gonna stop." He let his hands drop and was gone from the room before she dared open her eyes.

∗   ∗   ∗

Duke Wattiern DeLarouge sat comfortably before Gremlaw, picking at the plates of food on the table between them. Gremlaw had made his way to the liaison point after climbing the steps to Huleta's room and finding her gone. He was about to leave her a note to ask if she could keep watch over her mother until he recalled the fact that she could not read.

"Help yourself," DeLarouge stated in a cultured voice, gesturing to the food.

"Surely it's poisoned," Gremlaw retorted acidly.

DeLarouge turned up one corner of his mouth. "I must apologize for the methods we employed to get you here, but it is vital to the security of the kingdom that you cooperate." Receiving no reply, he continued, "As you must know, our neighbors in the empire of Lavash have been attempting to invade us for decades." DeLarouge paused for a response, continuing when one was not forthcoming. "My own dear father was lost in defense of the kingdom."

This time Gremlaw made an interjection. "So your father was killed in defense of the king, and you became a duke, while *my* father was killed building homes for the king, and I became a thief."

DeLarouge gazed at Gremlaw for a while, as if reassessing his thoughts regarding the younger man. "However, their previous attempts have been military in nature," DeLarouge went on, ignoring the remark. "Since we routed their forces three years past, this has changed." The duke paused to take a drink of red wine from a crystal goblet.

The room where they sat had been accessed through a long, below-ground tunnel that led from an obscured and locked door located in the same gaol from which Gremlaw had escaped. One of the watch's guards had led him through the blackness of the tunnel, a lantern their only source of light, with a second armed man bringing up the rear. The first guard had banged the hilt of his stubby sword against the thick wood of a door, the terminus of the passage, and walked silently away, leaving Gremlaw alone in the blackness.

Dark wood paneling clad the low-ceilinged room where Gremlaw had stood. Plush rugs covered the floor, and the table, which already had been laid with platters of food, was polished to a mirror-like sheen. Light was provided by hundreds of candles rather than lamps, and there was no fireplace, even though it was fairly warm inside. An ornately carved, plushly upholstered chair sat on either side of the table, and a single man, clad entirely in black, stood with his back to one wall. Gremlaw had seated himself on one of the chairs and casually helped himself to some meat and bread, staring at the guard who gave no reaction as he did so. Eventually DeLarouge had appeared, dressed in a similar fashion to the guard, and seated himself across from the younger man.

DeLarouge fixed Gremlaw with an intense stare. "We believe agents from Lavash are promoting the spread and use of a newly created narcotic known as 'Forever.' The drug is addictive from the first use, and so far, we have no information that anyone has been weaned from it. Users appear to have all their will taken from them. They become listless and ineffectual, their only goal being to obtain more Forever." DeLarouge paused before adding, "We've known about this drug for a little while. However, there have been some instances of it being used by members of the military who protect our borders from Lavash."

One of Gremlaw's eyebrows rose, as the kingdom's army was known for its harsh discipline and harsher punishments for breaches of it. "Did my supposed sister poison my mother with Forever?" he asked.

DeLarouge looked away before shaking his head.

Gremlaw paused for a while before adding, "Well, Duke, it's an interesting story and all, but what am I supposed to do about it? I'm a thief, not any kind of soldier."

Rather than provide an answer, DeLarouge rose and slid back one of the wooden panels that covered the walls, revealing a cavity beyond. From this space, he pulled a thick stack of papers then dropped it onto the table with a thump. "Have you any idea what this is?" he asked.

Gremlaw held up one hand and made a show of examining one of the papers from a few different angles. DeLarouge pursed his lips as the young man said, "I'll admit I'm no expert, Wattiern"—the duke scowled at the familiar use of his name—"but from what I *have* managed to come across in my poor existence, I'd say this is a sheaf of parchment."

An angry expression spread across the duke's face, and he reddened considerably. "What an extremely funny little boy you are," DeLarouge said acidly. "This is every single piece of intelligence I have on you!" Gremlaw's interest was piqued at this remark. "Everything my agents could find out about you: your past and present, friends and family. Everything." Gremlaw sniffed dismissively. "It has been noted you seem to have an uncanny ability to disappear while in plain sight," DeLarouge stated matter-of-factly. "If you indeed have this ability, it could be useful in finding out how the Lavashians are bringing this filth in."

Gremlaw felt he was being lured into a trap as he asked his next question. "Why would I help you?"

DeLarouge smiled the smile of a vicious predator. "It is not *I* you will be serving in this capacity." Gremlaw noted the certainty with which he spoke. "Your allegiance is to the crown—His Majesty the king—and the kingdom of Trathlain."

"You really must forgive me if I don't have quite the same sense of patriotic nationalism as you, Duke," Gremlaw stated sarcastically, "but the crown and the kingdom of Trathlain have done very little for me."

DeLarouge completely ignored Gremlaw's imitation of the duke's speech. The aristocrat and cousin to the king simply turned to the guard, who remained silent by the door. "I told you, Captain," he said. "I said this would be the response we would get." The captain maintained his silence and fixed stare. DeLarouge turned back to Gremlaw. "Of course, due to my anticipation of your response, certain other..." He paused, as if seeking the correct word. "Insurances,"—the duke nodded—"certain other insurances have been arranged."

Gremlaw took the bait. "Like what?"

"Your mother, Gremlaw. That young woman you so callously attempted to strangle? Terrible business that. Your own sister!" DeLarouge shook his head in mock disapproval. "You see, if you refuse to do as your king wishes, we'll have no recourse but to cease supplying her with the antidote to the poison we have administered." He sat back in his chair, a self-satisfied look of smugness on his face as he folded his arms. His expression altered somewhat, however, as Gremlaw's reply sank in.

"Let her die then." DeLarouge was shocked at the tone of his delivery more than his words. "My mother," Gremlaw added after a long pause, "died at the same time my father did. Her body simply did not recognize the fact." The young man sent a look of determined rage across the table. "It will be a relief for us both when her time comes." Gremlaw swallowed the lump that had formed in his throat as he realized these words were the truth.

DeLarouge shook his head and rested his arms on the table before speaking in a voice so quiet that Gremlaw had to lean forward too. "While that may be true, can the same be said for the flaxen-haired vixen who lives in the hovel above yours?" Gremlaw launched himself at DeLarouge, simultaneously lunging for his eyes and throat. Obviously not expecting such a move, neither DeLarouge nor the statuesque captain had enough time to react, and the lithe youth managed to clamp one hand on the duke's muscular throat. Gremlaw had not been able to blind the man as he wanted, so he resorted to smashing his fist into DeLarouge's face, hammering his arm up and down in a blur of rage-filled movements.

Oddly, the world exploded in a brilliant flash of light that began to fade into darkness before Gremlaw felt the agony in the back of his neck.

"Do not damage him!" It sounded as if DeLarouge shouted as Gremlaw felt his body crash into the stone wall before slumping to the cold floor. Groggy and disoriented, he shook his head and started to rise, leaning heavily on the wall for support. He looked sideways, where DeLarouge sat dabbing at his face with an elegantly embroidered, lace-trimmed silk handkerchief. The stoic captain stood a little to one side, his stare fixed unerringly upon Gremlaw.

"Intelligence reports stated you were fast," DeLarouge almost complimented. "I was not led to believe you could move *that* fast, however."

Gremlaw's head thumped with pain in time to his heartbeat, and a constant ache, which he could only think of as cold and white, jabbed the back of his neck. Despite his newfound agony, he dragged himself into a standing position and spat his words at the duke. "If Huleta is harmed in any way, I will spend my last breath taking yours."

DeLarouge stood. "Your mother is safe and being looked after," he stated simply. "Your girl is also safe and being well treated. Just do as we ask, and both shall be released unharmed. This I promise." Gremlaw felt the trap slam shut around him. "I understand you hate me," DeLarouge continued, "yet the security of this nation's borders is of paramount concern, and if I must resort to unpleasant, underhanded tactics, I will. No single individual is more important than the entire nation, and that includes myself." DeLarouge moved toward the panel that served as a door. "So will you assist us, or are your loved ones to die?" The duke paused for a few seconds before adding, "Your education begins tomorrow."

CHAPTER 4

G remlaw's back hit the dusty ground of the outdoor training arena, slivers of gravel slitting the flesh on his shoulder in dozens of places. He rolled backward, using the momentum of the fall to flip over and regain his feet. Since his meeting with Duke DeLarouge, he had spent most of his time being slapped around and punched to the ground by a monster of a man called "Dron," who seemingly had not much in the way of training. The brutish human, a questionable moniker at best, had originated in the semi-desert region known as Bruracame. His bronzed skin had been toughened by exposure to the harsh winds for which the area was known. Often carrying particles of sand, these winds could be deadly to the untrained, stripping the skin from a man and leaving him open to a slow death from infection. The thing, which had just hammered a fist the size of a grapefruit into Gremlaw, simply appeared to be a bulk of muscles; not an inch of fat separated the skin from the musculature, and thick veins bulged obscenely across various portions of his body. Dron's face was squashed, both down and inward, as if flattened from above and in front. His nose looked to have been snapped and reset so poorly and so often that it was barely recognizable as that organ. His shoulders and head seemed to meet without any need for the addition of a neck, and his massive legs set him in a permanent half squat. The overall impression Gremlaw originally had formed—that of a dimwitted, physically slow half human, half animal—had been quickly and brutally beaten out of him. Dron had a keen mind and could react fast enough to counter anything Gremlaw had tried so far.

"Again," Dron barked without any kind of inflection.

Gremlaw, still winded from the punch Dron had landed just below his sternum, found himself unable to stand completely upright and held his hand out to signal a halt. "Your enemies won't wait, boy," Dron sneered in a voice barely above a whisper. "They'll keep coming 'til you win, escape, or die." The brute of a man advanced on the youth, who backed off a few steps.

"Dron," Gremlaw gasped, "please." He noticed Dron pull something from a pocket in his loose-fitting trews and saw a short yet mean-looking club grasped in the ogre-like man's right hand. A cold rage surged through Gremlaw as he wondered why this vast man felt the need for a weapon. Surely, with fists the size of Gembrian ham hocks, he did not need one.

The change that took place within Gremlaw was not a particularly subtle event. Rage burned through him, restoring his ability to breathe, and he felt his consciousness shift into the awareness of negative space. Dron's form became fainter; a green outline against the backdrop of the world around him appeared, and Gremlaw's eyes, or mind, highlighted any spaces through which he would be able to dodge.

This time, however, time itself seemed to slow down for the young man. He became aware of Dron's movements, which appeared to be much slower than normal. Gremlaw noted the man's arm, the small club gripped in his fist as it was raised in a sharp arc of violence and brought toward his body. Gremlaw looked at his attacker's eyes, which flicked back and forth between his own eyes and a point just to the left of Gremlaw's chin. He knew! Gremlaw knew where the blow was aimed—directly for his left shoulder! Darting for the triangular space formed by Dron's upraised arm and muscular side, Gremlaw ducked beneath the attempted blow and turned around quickly to jump on the beast-like man's broad back. With the blade of his hand, Gremlaw made a slashing motion across Dron's bull neck and dropped to the ground, backing off a few steps in case the man took offense at his defeat.

The light breeze that swept a few leaves slowly across the ground returned to normal speed, as did the fluffy clouds, which made their lazy way across the sky once more, indicating that Gremlaw's state of consciousness had returned to normal too. Dron stood with his back to the youth as silence descended over the training grounds. Gremlaw wondered what response he might receive from the enormous man. Having no real frame of reference, even after three weeks of training, Gremlaw was unsure whether it might be anger or indifference, disappointment or elation, as Dron kept his emotions under tight control, if he had any.

Gremlaw waited quietly as his tutor turned slowly around with a solemn expression. The big man looked Gremlaw in the eye for at least a minute before a wide grin spread across his broken face. "Where did that come from, boy?" he asked animatedly. "I barely noticed you'd moved before I felt your fingers on my throat!"

Gremlaw managed to relax a little; this was the first hint of positivity he had received from Dron and surely must be a good sign. "I have no idea," he answered. "That hasn't happened to me before."

His tutor appeared to think for a second before gesturing to Gremlaw. "Come. We'll talk of this over a jug of cold beer."

Shocked at the immediate turnaround his teacher displayed, Gremlaw trotted across to where he stood. "Are we finished for the day then?" he asked.

Dron nodded and actually put his arm around Gremlaw's shoulder as the pair walked to the barrack-like building where Gremlaw had lived for the last six weeks. Thoughts of his mother and Huleta had almost been wiped from his mind during this time, as he had been so exhausted, physically and mentally, by the punishing routines he had endured.

"We're finished for good, Gremlaw." The younger man realized this was the first time Dron actually had called him by name. "If you can move as fast as you just did, I can't teach you any more."

The pair walked along a stone corridor with iron-barred cells along either side, one of which was Gremlaw's home, although at least these new quarters were unlocked even if his route to freedom was blocked. The building had a basic washroom with a well for drawing almost freezing water but offered little else. His food was delivered by either Dron or one of the black-clothed guards. Gremlaw took a final glance into the cell where he had slept and recovered.

The pair moved on as Dron added, "You know how to attack, how to defend, and you have speed on your side." To Gremlaw's relief, he withdrew his arm; it had felt like a heavy yoke upon him. "Your problem is going to be strength. Many people you'll face will be much stronger than you, so you'll to have to rely on speed to evade or defeat them." Gremlaw nodded at this remark.

Outside the barracks sat a number of other military-style constructs, yet there were no soldiers or recruits or seemingly anyone else at all. Gremlaw was unable to make out anyone's whereabouts in the city by looking at the towers and buildings beyond the compound they were in; he'd also been too disoriented from his meeting with DeLarouge and his captain to remember much of his arrival. When they approached a huge set of solid gates that barred their exit from the walled compound, Dron reached for a squared-off tree trunk that locked them in place. After heaving one end up as if it were made of paper, he allowed it to drop over and lean against one of the buildings before turning to Gremlaw once more.

"One final task, I think," he said while Gremlaw's face fell as fast as his hopes. "Get outside the gate, and we're done."

Gremlaw looked at the huge portal and sighed. He would be surprised if Dron could open it alone, let alone himself. He made a brief survey of the construction as his teacher leaned against the wall of a nearby building. The hinges had been fashioned to make the gate move inward, so pushing would be futile. There appeared to be no mechanical way for them to be opened, and at the thickness they looked to be, Gremlaw thought one of them must have weighed two or three tons.

He placed his hands on the bracket that supported the locking bar and gently leaned back, getting the expected result; the gate did not move, not even a tremble. Gremlaw scanned the area for a pole he could use as a lever, discounting the locking bar, as it would be too heavy, even though Dron had left it leaning against the wall of an interior building. Inspiration suddenly hit the young man, as he understood the purpose of this final test.

The athletic youth sprinted up to the locking bar, jumping at the last second to reach the roof of the building it leaned against. He found himself on the flat roof of the building and looked toward the outer wall of the compound, an easy jump for someone of his abilities. Crossing to the center of the roof, he sprinted headlong for the edge then launched himself toward the outer wall at the last possible second; the toes of his right foot connected with the sharp angle of the top of the wall. He experienced a feeling of freedom as he crossed the distance, landing with his left foot on top of the outer wall then dropping into a crouch. He allowed his right leg to crash sidelong into the inner surface of the wall, which acted like an anchor to ensure he didn't fall over the other side, and used his hands to help him balance. Outside the compound, he noticed a great bank of earth had been piled against the wall below where he perched, coming almost halfway up and topped with grass. Gremlaw lowered himself down the outside and, without hesitation, dropped to the small hill, rolling down the side as he hit the ground. After jumping to his feet, he trotted across to the outside of the gates where Dron now stood, obscured until now by a horse-drawn cart.

"Didn't think it would take you long," the big man complimented Gremlaw.

The young man saw, from the outside, that the gates had been fastened together, ensuring they never would open in the first place, and Gremlaw knew he had passed Dron or DeLarouge's final test. Looking to the other side of the gates he had just climbed, he saw a normal-size, plainly constructed door through which Dron must have come while he was performing his aerial stunts. Smiling, Gremlaw said, "Sneaky bunch, you lot."

"It's a sneaky business" was Dron's serious reply. "Up you get," he added in a more normal tone, indicating a small cart. "We've got some cool beer to sup."

Gremlaw felt a grip of fear in his belly as they hopped in and trundled away from the barracks, especially once he realized they were outside the city walls. Never before had Gremlaw been out of Palandine, and an almost agoraphobic panic threatened to settle in. He had lived within the walls before him for his whole life and the city inside had been his entire world. Yet, as he looked at it from a distance of about two miles, the capital city of the Trathlainian kingdom appeared to be small. If this place looked so small, he must be almost invisible in the vast, incomprehensible scope of the entire world. What possible difference could he make in a war between two kingdoms when a little distance reduced his known world? Gremlaw fought to control his breathing, and as the small cart crept toward the capital, he felt a reassuring hand clap his shoulder.

"You'll be good," Dron said, as if knowing what he was going through.

Dron steered the cart through various areas of Palandine, toward whatever his destination was. Gremlaw was under the impression they would be heading for a tavern or inn of some description, until the brute took him into one of the richest areas of the city. Palatial homes were surrounded by elegantly manicured formal gardens, some of which were quite large to be inside the city walls. Dron turned into one of the largest, most opulent looking properties and Gremlaw scanned the entire area as they approached the marbled facade with its carved columns and arched portico. Rather than halting before the entrance, however, Dron took the little cart down a paved road that led along the side of the building itself and to a more functional area at the rear. Here stablemen took charge of the horse and cart, bowing their heads respectfully to Dron as he thanked them each by name.

Beyond the stable area, a small path led the pair past flowering shrubs and tall trees that released a fresh floral scent into the air, a far cry from the stench of wood smoke and filth that pervaded the rest of Palandine. Gremlaw followed Dron through an archway that had been carved from a living hedge and found himself staring at the oddest-looking dwelling he'd ever encountered. Multi-hued and fashioned from some kind of cloth, the tented house was a semi-permanent construction with wooden walls to which layers of billowing cloth were attached. Pink, red, gold, blue, and numerous colors in between, the marquee was a riot of color and a distinct contrast to the other buildings in the compound. Behind this marquee stood the gray stone of the perimeter wall, twenty feet high and topped with vicious-looking spikes.

"A little piece of home," Dron explained. This must be what passed for housing in Bruracame, Gremlaw thought. "Come. Be welcome in my home," the beast-like man added, "but please remove your shoes before entering the main house." Gremlaw walked into what was essentially an antechamber to the main structure, with a simple bench on either side for use while he took off his shoes and a pair of racks in which to store them. Dron passed him a pair of light slippers that appeared to be made of silk and led him into the main house.

Astonishment overcame Gremlaw as he looked around the marquee. From the brightly polished wooden floors to the subtly decorated walls, everything—every inch—of the interior was ablaze with color. Far from being a riot, however, the hues blended and merged into one another, making Gremlaw feel as if he were standing in rainbow. Looking up, he noticed the colors came from the sunlight, which poured through the colored cloth that formed the roof. The young man had a little trouble reconciling the beauty of this home with the brutish, vicious man he had been exposed to for the past few weeks.

"This is beautiful, Dron," Gremlaw whispered, still in awe.

"And I am not," Dron stated with a wry twist of his lips. "DeLarouge finds it gaudy, which is why we're stuck at the rear of his grounds behind a tall hedge." So, Gremlaw thought, the massive stone fortress they had passed was the ducal palace of DeLarouge.

"Husband!" a female voice piped up as a figure entered from one of the side rooms. Gremlaw could tell it was a woman from the way the brown robe clung to her at hip and breast. "You home sooner." Her accent was unusual and one Gremlaw could not readily place. He was further hindered in his identification of this woman as she was completely concealed in a brown, hooded robe that fell to her ankles and below which she wore a pair of silk slippers like the ones both Gremlaw and Dron wore.

"Mishu," Dron greeted his wife warmly. "I have missed your presence by my side." This last sounded, to Gremlaw, like a formal greeting rather than a heartfelt statement. "This is Gremlaw, our student." Dron turned. "Gremlaw, this is my wife, Mi-Zhu-Quan."

"You call 'Mishu,'" the woman said as she bowed her head to the young man.

Gremlaw hesitated for a second until he remembered his manners. "I—It's an honor to make your acquaintance, Mishu," he stammered.

"Surprise?" she asked in her unusual accent.

Gremlaw blushed but answered anyway, "A little, Mishu, yes. This man, who it turns out is married"—Gremlaw indicated Dron, who was smiling—"has spent the past six weeks beating me to the ground and calling me names." Gremlaw grunted a laugh. "Now I find he is married and lives inside a rainbow!" Dron and Mishu laughed at this. "It's all more than a bit strange." He shrugged as an apology.

"Come," Mishu instructed. "Comforts to be provided."

Gremlaw followed the couple into another area, which had a low table in the center, surrounded by plushy upholstered cushions.

"You guest here," Mishu told Gremlaw. "Please to sit." The young man did as requested as Dron continued into another area of the massive tent.

The big man returned shortly with a huge tray, upon which sat a large cream-colored jug and two metal tankards, along with fruit, bread, and cheese. He poured Gremlaw a tankard of dark-brown beer and passed it across as his student studied Mishu a little more. Her hood obscured her face with a combination of the cloth and shadow, revealing nothing more than her chin and lower lip. The latter was a deep-red color and looked to be quite plump; further than this, Gremlaw could make out nothing. He watched as Dron sat next to his wife, who leaned into him and placed one of her long-fingered hands on his crossed leg. Gremlaw felt a little awkward at this outward display of affection. In the society in which he had been raised, it was frowned upon. Gremlaw concentrated on his drink and took some of the cheese at Dron's nod.

"You don't have any servants?" Gremlaw asked to break the awkward silence.

"In my country," Dron replied, "you're considered a bad host if you allow someone else to serve your guests."

Gremlaw nodded slowly, "And in your country, Mishu?" he asked, drinking. Gremlaw noticed the woman stiffen, and a hard line formed on the portion of her mouth he could see.

"Some have slaves," she answered.

Unfortunately this information did not provide Gremlaw enough of a clue as to where she was from; silence descended over them once more.

"Well, it would seem I've hit a nerve," Gremlaw observed in a light tone. "So I might as well just come out and ask. Where are you from, Mishu?"

The couple glanced at each other, and it was Dron who answered. "Mishu defected from the empire of Lavash about twenty years ago, Gremlaw." He added quietly, "She doesn't like to speak about it."

"I'm sorry," Gremlaw stated. Now he knew why he had been unable to identify where Dron's wife was from. She came from the country Trathlain was at war with. He changed his line of questioning. "Dron introduced me as 'our student.' Does that mean you'll be teaching me something too?"

Her lip formed a smile. "Husband Dron say you have quick mind," she said. "He not say how quick you be. I user of magic," Mishu said, as if it were the most ordinary thing in the world.

Gremlaw snorted. "Magic! I'm hardly a child to be told tales of magic!"

Dron reddened but remained silent while his wife continued in her quiet voice, "Magic rare, yes, but in Lavash a few can use."

With a sense of wonder, Gremlaw looked from one to the other; they were both deadly serious. He decided to play along. "Well then," he said as he drained his tankard, "when will we start?"

* * *

Mishu rose with the morning sun and summoned Gremlaw to her. "Walk with me," she said as she left the tent. Gremlaw followed her after putting on his boots. He had been left in a small room with a low bed and provided with some clothes that somehow fit him perfectly. They wandered aimlessly through DeLarouge's garden, Mishu apparently looking for something only she knew existed.

Finally, they reached a stone seating area, surrounded by trees, where Mishu sat. "Have sit," she said. Gremlaw smiled at her accent and poor linguistic skills; even if she did believe in magic, she was a nice person. "Remember yesterday when you come here new?" she asked. Gremlaw nodded. "Think it now. Tell what seen."

Gremlaw made a list of objects, locations, colors, and even the things he had smelled as Dron had brought him to the rear of the house and the tent they shared. "Good. Now not think. Answer." Gremlaw nodded. "How many windows front of house have got?"

He closed his eyes to concentrate. "Twelve."

"How many steps lead to door?"

"Eight."

This question-and-answer session continued, with Gremlaw getting each question right, even as they became progressively more obscure. Eventually Mishu stopped asking questions.

"Mishu, I don't see how this will help me learn magic."

The woman sniffed. "Not can *teach* magic, teach how *feel* when other person use magic." She clarified, "Close eyes again. Feel. Feel air, ground, seat, trees round you." Gremlaw tried to do as she asked, tried to make himself aware of his surroundings as a bird flew overhead. "You feel?"

Gremlaw nodded. "I think so."

"Now feel this." Her voice sounded as if it came from inside his head—in his brain or consciousness. A slight tingle began between his shoulder blades, making Gremlaw aware of something, something out of place or wrong. The tingling spread up and forward, around the skin of his neck and into his throat, which tightened a little. He shook his head as if to dislodge the feeling and realized he no longer could feel anything of the rest of the world; all he could concentrate on was the tingling. He opened his eyes to see what was happening and looked upon Mishu, who was surrounded by a pale-blue glow. Fright pulsed into Gremlaw as she radiated the blue light. He recoiled off the stone bench, backing away from her.

"This what magic feel like!" Mishu shouted inside Gremlaw's mind, which made him back away even more. As if a thread had been cut, the feeling crawling through his entire scalp, along with the blue glow, vanished, returning the world to how it had been before.

"Magic not for children story," the Lavashian woman said in a dismissive tone.

Gremlaw swallowed and tried to calm his breathing. "No," he managed to splutter, "it's not! What was that?" he asked, remaining where he was.

Mishu patted the bench beside her. "Not hurt you," she reassured him. "What I do is shield," she added from the depths of her cowl.

Gremlaw made his cautious way over and sat next to her again. "A shield?" he asked, puzzled. "It didn't look much like a shield to me."

Mishu's head snapped around to stare at him from the dark depths of her hood. "What mean?" she demanded.

"All that blue light around you didn't look like any shield I've ever seen," Gremlaw explained.

Mishu shook her head, which made the cloth shift around her. "No light! Magic not be seen!" she stated vehemently.

Gremlaw looked into the depths of the cowl that covered her face and shrugged. "Mishu," he began gently, "I'm not trying to make you cross, but when I opened my eyes and saw you, it looked as if a pale-blue light was coming from inside you." He spoke slowly to make sure the Lavashian woman understood him.

Mishu looked at the ground for a few seconds before asking, "Gremlaw frighten if Mishu read mind?"

"Damn right I'd be frightened," he said, "but I think I trust you enough to have a look in here."

As if this were her cue, Mishu grabbed his hand and dragged him toward her home. "Come!" she shouted as Gremlaw laughed. "Come now!"

Mishu asked Gremlaw to lie on the bed he had slept in and make himself comfortable. She had told Dron what was about to happen and asked him to bring some fruit juice and bread. She explained to Gremlaw that she'd never had much success in performing this particular feat before, as her talents had led toward generating the shield.

"Each one," she explained, "has special magic they do best. Train for this and nothing other." The Lavashian added, "Be calm. Not hurt you." Gremlaw noticed an impish smile form on the one lip he could see. "Feel funny." Mishu settled herself next to the prone youth. Then she reached one of her long-fingered hands toward his head and gently placed it on his forehead.

Almost immediately, Gremlaw felt the tingle begin at the back of his neck. Mishu's hand was like ice on his head, yet there was no pain, as she had promised. Abruptly his sense of self—his awareness—was pushed aside, as if something were trying to get into his brain. Gremlaw always had felt that the part of him that was his soul, if he had one, or consciousness, lived inside his head, just above his nose and between his eyebrows. Whatever resided there was being forcibly moved—pushed and shifted—as if to make room for another. Mishu was right; it did feel odd. His mind now felt as if it were located above his left eye, and he felt a sensation of *otherness* above his right.

Next came a gentle merging of this other mind with his. Gremlaw's mind was being directed, with exquisite gentleness, to recall the events it could concerning Gremlaw, Mishu, and his introduction to magic. Gremlaw was fascinated by this experience. He was watching as an external force manipulated his mind into remembering specific events. It appeared to him as if Mishu could view a single memory, like a picture in a book, or the entire sequence of an event as a whole. Eventually the iconic image of Mishu's body radiating pale-blue light was brought to the front of both minds and held there while the Lavashian woman explored it. At this exact moment, ice-cold pain lanced Gremlaw's brain, spearing into Mishu's head too.

Dron noticed his wife and Gremlaw stiffen at the same time. Mishu's breathing became labored, and Gremlaw's all but stopped as his body arched up from the bed, vibrating at an appalling rate. The man had no idea what to do; he and Mishu had linked minds hundreds of times, especially during lovemaking, as it increased the close bond they shared, and nothing had ever gone wrong. He laid a hand on his wife's shoulder and nearly shouted in fright at the rock-hard, tense muscles he felt. Feeling her arms and hands, Dron discovered she was as rigid as Gremlaw appeared to be. Having no real idea how Mishu performed her magic, Dron did not want to pull her hand from the young man's head in case it caused damage to one or both of them. Having no other solution, Dron knelt behind the woman he loved and whispered into her ear. His whispers covered the scope and depth of his love for her and how life would be a soulless abyss without her. He needed her and wanted her to come back.

Sealed in a world of agony, Gremlaw barely could function. He could just sense that Mishu's mind bore into the depths of his memory like a worm burrowing its way through a corpse. Thoughts and feelings, sights and sounds—nothing seemed to be sacred to this Lavashian—and hatred formed inside him; this race was not to be trusted for any reason. The pain felt like a bolt of white-hot lightning cutting into his brain, searing his mind as she plundered her way through Gremlaw's past, sucking information into her own memory as she did so. Fear and horror drove Gremlaw to seek some kind of sanctuary from the pain and the awful ripping feeling inside his mind. A less than subtle change jerked both minds back up through the depths of Gremlaw's memory, from his infant recollections of his father, past his mother and her loss of sanity, to his meeting of Huleta when they were still children and her more recent rejection of him. Up through the remembrance of each theft, of every feeling of guilt, elation, sadness, and joy, the joined minds soared until they returned to their respective positions above each of his eyes.

Gremlaw felt tremendous relief as he realized the experience was over, and this woman had managed to take everything she had wanted, or had been *instructed*, to take. This relief was short-lived, however, as Gremlaw felt his mind being dragged *through* his skull. Still linked with Mishu's mind, his mind was being sucked from inside his brain, pulled out of his head, and into her hand. The panic he felt was almost palpable as he tried in vain to stay inside his own body. Frantically Gremlaw tried to hold on with hands of thought to the last piece of him he could identify. His grip was broken, however, and linked with her, his mind shot toward her brain.

A sense of triumph coursed through Gremlaw's consciousness as he found himself slammed deep into her myriad of memories. Mishu was almost double Gremlaw's age, however, and her memories ran a great deal deeper than his. She remembered vague human shapes that had feelings of love attached, and these she believed to be her parents. Her feelings changed a little later as she was forcibly removed from these blurred people and taken to a place filled with harshness and brutality. Mishu had been forced to use her magic by people for whom she had no love and who only wanted to use her power for their own ends. As her life progressed, Gremlaw witnessed countless atrocities and abuses wrought against her, culminating in her forced pregnancy. Even though her baby had been brought upon her by violation, she developed a mother's love for her daughter, but after a happy year, during which Mishu had been left alone, the baby had been cruelly ripped from her.

Gremlaw felt something inside him snap painfully as he experienced this memory, and although he was unaware of it, his body shed tears for the loss of this child. Both linked minds experienced the deep depression Mishu had suffered after she had learned her daughter had died. Survivor's guilt and sorrow had mingled within Mishu until her mind had almost broken itself with the endless thoughts. Hate eventually took over, however, and Mishu had lashed out at the mind of the man who kept her locked away, severing the connections that held his mind inside his brain and killing him instantly, allowing her to escape.

The memories flooded from her mind into his. Everything Mishu recalled from that day until this moment was packed into Gremlaw's mind, leaving him reeling. The final few images, thoughts, and feelings were concerned with this very event and conveyed her agony, shock, and surprise at what was happening. No matter what Gremlaw had believed about her, Mishu had no ill will while rifling through his memories and had suffered as badly as he had. Gremlaw felt a surge of pity for this woman who had been treated so horrifically by her own countrymen. His mind seemed to peel apart from Mishu's, and he felt himself flow back down her neck and arm, through her hand, and back into his own brain.

Dron felt his diminutive wife jolt, as if some massive force had hit her, then collapse into his arms like a pole-axed animal. He cradled her, stroking her face as she filled her lungs and let out a scream that made his blood run cold. Mishu yelled a cry filled with the deepest despair her husband ever had heard, and his heart broke to hear it. Gremlaw had curled into a fetal position on the bed and was cradling his head tightly in his arms.

"Mishu, what happened?" Dron asked his sobbing wife.

Mishu's mouth opened and closed as if she were trying to speak, yet no words issued forth. Dron could only hold her and rock her backward and forward in the hope she eventually would recover.

Gremlaw slept until the evening shadows had robbed the interior of the tent of all its color and Dron had lit a number of lamps that gave off a gentle yet subdued glow. He awoke slowly, allowing the aches throughout his body and in his head to register before finally opening his eyes. Feeling as if he had been soundly beaten from head to foot, he gingerly rose to his feet and stumbled out of the room in which he had been left. He moved into the adjacent room to find Dron and Mishu relaxing among the cushions.

They turned to look at him when he entered. "How do you feel?" Mishu asked. Gremlaw was shocked, as she had asked her question in perfectly accentless Trathlainian.

"Got to admit, I've felt better, Mishu. What happened to your accent?"

She looked down. "It must have been something to do with what happened to us earlier."

"Yes," Gremlaw stated. "What exactly *did* happen to us?"

Mishu shook her head. "I'm sorry, Gremlaw. Really I am. I don't have any idea why the link went as wrong as it did."

Gremlaw thought for a moment. "I remember everything about your life, as if I lived it myself," he said in a subdued tone.

To his surprise, Mishu removed her hood and looked him directly in the eyes. "I recall your life as if it were mine too."

Her hair was so black it appeared to have violet streaks running through it. Her pale-skinned face had high cheekbones and a thin nose, but the most striking feature was her eyes. They were enormous and almost perfectly round; the dark-blue irises were huge as well and surrounded oval, catlike pupils. Gremlaw's examination of her striking face was disturbed by Duke DeLarouge, who entered the tent after calling for permission.

"Gremlaw," he began without any other preamble or greeting, "I have arranged for someone to take you downriver on a goods barge, and I require you to leave immediately."

CHAPTER 5

Nausea rose in Gremlaw as the carriage clattered along the city streets. DeLarouge studied the youth momentarily. "The ship will be headed north for the port of Silverdane," he stated. "Once there, you are to head to the Broken Mast, a tavern near the dockside, and ask for a man called 'Semmental.' He's been keeping the area under observation for a while now and can bring you up to speed on the situation as well as some new information he has discovered."

Gremlaw sensed more than understood that he was supposed to make some comment. "Semmental," he croaked, "at the Broken Mast."

DeLarouge nodded sharply, as if satisfied. "The owner of the river-boat has a few items and some coins for you. Make sure you take every-thing he gives you." Gremlaw nodded wordlessly.

As the carriage pulled to a clattering halt, he could tell from the sound of the horses' hooves that they were on a wooden surface. DeLarouge opened the door to the carriage, a much less decorated af-fair than the duke usually rode in, and climbed down the few steps to the dockside. Urging Gremlaw along the quay, he paused next to what looked to be a half-rotten, half-sunk river barge with a mound of crates, bags, and barrels in the center, all covered with a large tarpaulin.

Gremlaw dubiously looked at the mass of floating boards. "Lucky I learned to swim," he muttered, almost to himself.

DeLarouge's hearing was better than he had expected, however, as he replied, "You will be perfectly safe aboard this vessel, Gremlaw." The duke shifted position and spoke quietly. "Semmental can get a message to me and I to him. You and I are to have no contact. From this point on, you are on your own. Semmental will inform you of the details. He knows more regarding the situation in Silverdane than I." DeLarouge paused as if considering what to say next.

As he turned to make his way back to the carriage, Gremlaw gripped his arm and hissed, "If I make it back from this, I'm going to cut your throat as you sleep."

DeLarouge turned to see the hatred radiating from Gremlaw's eyes and replied sadly, "Get in line, Gremlaw. There are hundreds who would see me dead, and they are almost all more powerful and resourceful than *you*." Then he walked away from the young man.

"That may be, Dukey," Gremlaw called, "but can they make themselves almost invisible?" DeLarouge continued to walk along the dock as Gremlaw turned and hopped into the wallowing barge, looking for the owner in the dark.

The King's Own was not a name Gremlaw would have associated with the rotting woodpile that was his downriver conveyance. *Flotsam* came to mind as a new name, yet Gremlaw held his tongue as the bulky man who owned *The King's Own* appeared fanatically protective of the boat. He stood in the stern, one meaty hand on the tiller arm as the ancient barge meandered downstream in the current.

"A fine vessel she be," Hartsen told Gremlaw. "Brung me wealth and good fortune aboth."

Gremlaw nodded, although this appeared to be as far from the truth as possible. If this boat had made him rich, Hartsen had not invested any of it back into *The King's Own*. The man himself wore ragged, badly patched clothes that were stained and dirty. No, Gremlaw decided, this was definitely a fiction in Hartsen's mind.

"I was told you had some things for me," the young man said.

"Yap," Hartsen said in his obviously affected accent. "Small chest aforedecks. Ya canna miss it." With this, he fell silent.

Clambering toward the bow, Gremlaw searched in the semidarkness, eventually stumbling across what looked to be the only chest in the entire section. After flipping the lid, he found his eyes barely could penetrate the inky interior as the barge had passed beyond the city walls, and clouds obscured the stars. Deciding to wait until daylight, Gremlaw tried to make himself comfortable and soon drifted into the place between sleep and wakefulness, where imagination is most heightened. While he was aware of the slap of water against wood and the occasional bird-call, his thoughts turned to Huleta and the number of situations she might be held. His subconscious mind conjured a wide range of scenarios, from her being chained and left to rot in a dark cell, to another where she had met someone else and fallen in love with him, forgetting Gremlaw entirely. He shifted uncomfortably as these quasi dreams played across his mind. He eventually jerked awake as a faceless figure rammed a rusty spike into Huleta's stomach; his brain painted a vivid picture of her beautiful face contorted in agony.

In the silver light of predawn, Gremlaw opened the chest again. Inside lay an expensively made yet used cloak as black as coal inside and out. Beneath this, he found a small purse with some low-value coins inside, a long dagger or short sword—depending on your interpretation—and a small leather bag that could be slung over one shoulder. Within the waterproofed bag was a map of northern Trathlain with the border between it and the empire of Lavash highlighted along with a number of other features, such as trade routes used by the Durana Trading Company and all the garrison towns along the border. Instantly Gremlaw noticed the Durana routes led, more often than not, to one or more of the border garrison towns. Having never traveled farther than the training center with Dron, Gremlaw had little idea of the layout of the rest of the country, let alone the world, and found himself fascinated by this piece of parchment with its carefully described and colored markings, drawings, and symbols. Eventually he replaced the map and took out the other item inside the small bag, a letter.

Brief hope swelled in Gremlaw's chest as he thought this might be a letter DeLarouge had allowed him from Huleta. He broke the plain wax seal to scan the words, only to find they were from the duke. Although he knew Huleta was illiterate, he had wondered if she could dictate her words to a scribe or some other person of education, yet DeLarouge had denied him even this. Gremlaw read its vague contents, as his parents had taught him to do years before.

G,

Once you reach the seaport, passage has been booked in your name aboard a spice trader called Scent from Heaven. *Remain hidden while aboard, and let as few people as possible know your real name. Use a fake name if need be. Once you reach Silverdane, make for the inn I mentioned and find your contact there.*
—D

Nothing else had been added—the whole note had been left deliberately vague—and Gremlaw ripped it into small pieces before scattering it into the river. He examined the cubit-long blade and sheath before strapping the dagger to his side, leaving the handle just below his left armpit, thereby concealing the weapon once the cloak was on. He slung the light bag, now with the purse inside, over his head and one shoulder, then wrapped the black cloak around his shoulders and fastened it at his throat.

*   *   *

The King's Own made it to the Trathlainian seaport of Gabech on the eastern coast on the afternoon of their second day of travel.

Divine grace alone had prevented the thing from sinking, Gremlaw thought as he climbed a rope ladder to the dock planking above. He bade a brief farewell to Hartsen, who virtually had ignored him during the whole trip although he could speak to his barge as if it were sentient.

Gremlaw's first impression was that Gabech stank. Situated on both banks of the wide mouth of the Gabechian River and catering to numerous barges, sloops, and sailing ships, the city offered a mingling of cultures, businesses, and waters all mixed to create a rotten stench Gremlaw could not get out of his nostrils. The river and brackish waters mixed here and contained any number of waste products from the town around it. Rotting fish and other dead animals, combined with decomposing vegetation and sewage, produced a sulfuric, acrid, possibly poisonous smell. *How do people live here?* Gremlaw wondered as he made his way along the dock toward the larger ships. Adding to his overall disgust with the town, sailors and porters, hawkers and hookers mingled in every space and shouted over one another in vain attempts to be heard. Although Gremlaw had been raised in a city, there were only a few areas of Palandine that had no street cleaners, and it came as a culture shock to realize not everywhere was as clean as his home city. The young man made his way along the quayside, farther away from the river and toward the larger seagoing vessels.

Approaching an official-looking man who stood in the center of the stone walkway that allowed access and egress to the international docks, Gremlaw asked, "Could you direct me to a ship called *Scent from Heaven*, sir?" He affected a subservient, fawning manner of speech, hoping it would make him less memorable.

The harbor master looked at Gremlaw as if he were something unpleasant he had trodden in and gruffly ordered, "Out the way, boy. There be men's work to do."

Gremlaw tried to pass him, but the man stopped him and roughly shoved him back. The young man scouted the area to see whether there was another way to get into this area of the docks. His route, however, was entirely blocked by high walls and the original construction of the docks themselves.

Gremlaw sat down and studied the actions of the man and the pair of lackeys who now backed up his authority with swords. The first apparent aspect of the man's behavior was his corrupt nature. Gremlaw knew next to nothing about the function this man served, yet he realized it had something to do with money, as a few of the well-dressed ship captains seemed more than happy to give this self-important man purses of cash. This told Gremlaw there was either smuggling or tax avoidance going on, with the assistance of an agent of the king. Devious plans formed in Gremlaw's mind until he thought about his need to remain inconspicuous.

His train of thought took an abrupt about-face, and he decided to try to shift his conscious thought into the place where he could see negative space. Gremlaw attempted to coax his mind to alter, tried to recall what he had seen and felt as he had raced through the streets back home, all to no avail. Once, he thought his perception was about to shift, but his vision only blurred for a few seconds before returning to normal. After more than two hours of watching the harbor master take bribes and push people about, and failing to see negative space, Gremlaw was about to give up and ask about the ship in the local taverns and inns. One final thought sprung into his mind, however; the two previous times he had seen the green outlines around the negative spaces, he had been running, his blood pumping and adrenaline coursing through his body. He knew what he had to do.

Taking off at a leisurely jog, Gremlaw set a course away from the docks, dodging people and animals, carts and crates. He climbed a steep hill—littered with odd-looking houses and other less identifiable buildings—and halted at the top to look down upon the port. Gremlaw tried to summon the thought that he was being chased by the watch or a faceless villain intent on spilling his blood, then set off at a sprint.

Past homes and businesses he raced, past wide-eyed men and open-mouthed women staring at his mad dash, and past laughing children, delighted to see his antics. Elation swelled in the young man as he charged headlong toward the most heavily trafficked portion of town.

Tunnels appeared as his vision adapted and changed to detect the negative spaces in between the objects that surrounded them. Pale-green light limned the perimeter of each as he darted for the first gap, between two groups of people who were either bartering or arguing. Gremlaw nearly laughed as the two groups finally noticed him charging directly toward them, their faces transforming into expressions of shock as he slipped easily between them. He dove under and between the wheels of a large cart laden with barrels, sliding and rolling sideways until he regained his feet to continue, barely slowed by the maneuver.

With the malodorous wind in his hair and on his face, Gremlaw plunged directly for the harbor master. Due to the nature of his sight, Gremlaw did not have to dodge and weave around people in a haphazard fashion; rather the green-lined spaces seemed to link up in his mind and provide him with the fastest route, even if the people who were forming the negative spaces moved. Gremlaw hit the stone dock of the quayside at all his fullest speed, arms pumping and with a grimace that was a combination of a grin and his exertions.

Ten feet from the three men who blocked the wharves beyond, someone shouted as he raced past him, just knocking his arm. This call alarmed the harbor master, whose eyes widened in horror as he turned to see the apparition that was descending on him. He had forgotten the boy from earlier whom he had dismissed so easily, and in truth Gremlaw looked very little like he had then. His face wore a grin, which the harbor master took for a murderous snarl, and his black cape streamed behind him like the wings of a demonic being.

The harbor master obviously had a guilty conscience, as he promptly dropped to his knees and covered his head with his hands, crying, "Save me!" in a high-pitched voice to the pair of armored guards who accompanied him.

Too slow, the guards clumsily drew their weapons and turned to face the madman who was racing toward his death. They seemed to think if they simply leveled their swords in his direction, Gremlaw would impale himself. Gremlaw, however, had other plans. He reached the trio and jumped forward, his leading foot connecting sharply against the back of the cowering harbor master, using him like a living springboard. He vaulted over the guards, tucking his legs into a midair crouch to avoid hitting their bunched shoulders, and landed hard on the cobbles beyond. Gremlaw stumbled and almost fell but managed to right himself before plunging toward the ships, losing himself between massive hulls and piles of boxed cargo.

Of the eight ships docked in this area of the harbor, the one Gremlaw wanted was the farthest away from the harbor master and his brutes, and despite the name *Scent from Heaven*, the whole ship reeked of tar, salt, and fish. Gremlaw had no idea whether to just walk onto the ship or call first, yet he wished to remain hidden from any pursuit. He walked alongside the ship from stern to bow, wondering at the skill and craftsmanship that had gone into its construction.

* * *

Although he was a city man, Gremlaw did well aboard the small ship as it coasted northward on a gentle breeze. He suffered no sickness whatsoever and earned some respect from the crew by scurrying up and down the ratlines as if he had been at sea his whole life.

A familiar stench rose from the seawater around Silverdane, the product of the large amounts of rotting fish offal and rubbish the populace threw into the sea. Gremlaw noticed the poor construction used in building the waterfront properties: thick wooden beams, clad in planks and coated in tar for protection against the vicious effects of the seawater. As far as the eye could see, black-coated buildings formed the unpleasant little town that was half the size of the port at Gabech. Gremlaw bid farewell to the captain of *Scent from Heaven* and walked along the tarred timbers of the dockside.

Not knowing the layout of the town, he drew his cloak around him to protect himself from the evening chill and set out along the waterfront. Pedestrian traffic was surprisingly light as Gremlaw wended his way past taverns, inns, warehouses, and shops, although he was propositioned by no fewer than three women asking if he wanted company. Finally reaching the farthest end of the waterfront, where this section of the town ceased, Gremlaw was about to make his way inland to continue his search when he noticed what constituted little more than a shack jammed between two larger buildings. He smiled as he saw the snapped mast of a ship that leaned against this shed, which appeared even shoddier than the rest of the buildings along the waterfront.

He entered the Broken Mast and scanned the room in which he found himself. Rough-hewn tables and chairs had been placed, seemingly at random, throughout the fairly large room, which was poorly lit with smoky lamps burning whale fat. The smell was almost sickening to Gremlaw, and he wondered how people could eat in here. Most of the chunky furniture was occupied by depressingly poor sailors with scabbed hands and weather-beaten faces. Not one of them took notice of the new entrant as he made his way to the bar, which was little more than a large chunk of driftwood perched atop some crates.

"Help ye?" a pockmarked man asked. He had tried to hide his balding head with the age-old technique of pulling nine strands of hair across his greasy scalp. Badly shaven, hanging jowls wobbled as his broken-toothed mouth worked. Patched and food-stained, his clothing reminded Gremlaw of the items rag pickers tried to pass off as clothing in Palandine.

"I'm looking for Semmental," Gremlaw told the barkeep.

"Take ye a seat," the man replied, waving a flabby arm around the room. "He'll not be in for some time yet. Do ye need ale or food?"

"Just ale," Gremlaw stated. He could not begin to think about eating something prepared by this man or in this place. He retreated to the darkest corner of the commons to begin the wait for his contact.

CHAPTER 6

Gremlaw sat with his back to the rough wall of the inn, sipped at the seawater that passed for ale here, and waited for Semmental. After what seemed like hours and two unsatisfying tankards of ale later, an emaciated, bow-backed man of middling years slipped in from the side entrance. He sidled across to the barkeep, who cut his eyes briefly toward Gremlaw as this newcomer spoke. The man Gremlaw thought was Semmental turned to look at the youth, who made brief eye contact before returning to his watery ale. Surveying the room over the rim of the rough wooden tankard the ale was served in, Gremlaw noted the inn was beginning to fill with sailors and dockworkers and was becoming crowded and rowdy. Semmental glanced at Gremlaw once more and raised his eyebrows before exiting the establishment. This was all the incentive Gremlaw needed to leave the place, yet he made sure he finished his drink before following Semmental outside.

Detritus and rotting garbage filled the alley Gremlaw found himself in. The stench was overpowering as he cast his glance around, taking note of all available exits. There were few. One end led back to the waterfront, its opposite away, and there was no sign of Semmental. Gremlaw opted to put the waterfront at his back and head into the maze of the town. A whisper of movement to his left caused him to duck right, into a space formed by a black shadow and broken crates. Semmental was blundering around like a toddler in the alley, tripping over the mess of human rubbish scattered there. He was dressed in a ragged, faded coat and tattered leggings of some thin cloth. Gremlaw could see a good portion of his lower legs and ankles, which were stick thin. He moaned inwardly; *this* was to be his contact? The sight would have been funny under other circumstances; now his life depended on this odd character.

"Semmental," Gremlaw said, as he stepped from his concealment. The other man screamed in such a high-pitched manner that Gremlaw feared people would come looking for a woman in distress. "We should go," he said to Semmental, who clutched his chest in fright. The man led Gremlaw through the streets and alleys of Silverdane, his stooped body staggering along at an almost recreational pace. Eventually the wraith-like man led Gremlaw toward a rundown plank building with one grimy, cracked windowpane to view the world, like a Cyclops's eye. Gremlaw would rather have stayed outside, yet Semmental slipped through the unlocked door.

Once inside, Semmental performed some kind of routine, checking several areas in a ritualistic manner. The older man glanced at Gremlaw and flashed his eyebrows up once before almost completely transforming into a different man. His stoop disappeared, and he ran his hands through his hair, pulling it back to tame the mass of graying strands. The vacant look left his eyes as he completed the transformation. Even his shoddy clothing seemed not quite as worn out as it had before.

"I came across some information," Semmental told Gremlaw. Although he spoke softly, his high-pitched voice was a grating experience on the ear. "I managed to find out who's responsible for distributing Forever inside the kingdom."

"And?" Gremlaw asked, tilting his head and raising one eyebrow.

Semmental looked disappointed as he answered, "Fitlock Haguana. Took control of the Durana Trading Company about ten years ago. It was legitimately run until three years past." He spread his hands in a slight shrug. "Word is, agents from Lavash took the man's family as insurance against his good behavior."

Gremlaw felt an instant familiarity with this Haguana character; after all, he had been treated in the same way. He sighed and looked around the worn-out, dingy hut. "Nice place you have here," he said dryly.

Semmental smiled, revealing a row of twisted, rotten, blackened teeth. "All part of the disguise, my friend," he stated, gesturing to himself with one arm. "All part of the disguise." His face took on a puzzled expression. "How did the big man get you to work for him?" he asked.

Gremlaw eyed him suspiciously, wondering whether this was some sort of trap DeLarouge had set up to see whether he would reveal anything about himself. *I couldn't care less*, Gremlaw thought. "He's got my ma and a very good friend of mine under arrest. He says he'll kill them both if I don't do this."

Semmental shook his head. "Rotten bastard!" he shouted, surprising Gremlaw, as no one else had voiced such opinions. "Devious, underhanded, motherless bastard!" Semmental brought his fist crashing down on the small table before turning to Gremlaw. "It's what he does," the thin man continued in a calmer tone, "uses people like they're disposable commodities to be wasted at his own whim." Semmental's face took on a look of despair.

"Go on then," Gremlaw encouraged. "What's your story?"

Semmental grunted a bitter laugh. "My story, eh?" He took a deep breath. "Our mutual employer"—he said the last word in a sarcastic tone—"found me holed up in the seediest of seedy gambling houses in Palandine. I'd had several runs of good luck, made a small fortune." His damp eyes glazed over at the reminiscence. "Needless to say, I got greedy and lost every last copper." Here Semmental swallowed hard. "I...I ended up borrowing money from the wrong kind of men, and a price was put on my head when I couldn't pay them back. I'd lost it all..." He trailed off, obviously meaning he had lost far more than just money. The skinny man snapped out of his reverie and fixed Gremlaw with a look filled with self-loathing. "Then *he* turned up with a purse full of money and said he was willing to pay off my debts if I did some work for him. He made it abundantly clear if my answer was no, he'd happily turn me over to the men I owed."

Gremlaw nodded. "Left you no choice then."

Semmental nodded and examined the backs of his hands. "So I got shipped out here, miles from nowhere, and charged with the valuable job of keeping tabs on your new friend Haguana."

"My new friend," Gremlaw said slowly, as if trying out the words. "Well, you'd better tell me as much as you know, and I'll have a look at what he gets up to each day."

Semmental had been keeping an eye on Fitlock Haguana for quite some time, so he had a great deal of information on the Durana Trading Company and the man who ran the enterprise. Haguana lived alone now that Lavashians had abducted his wife and daughters. He told people who asked after them that they had gone to stay with his wife's mother, who had been ill for some time. As for his daily routine, Haguana seemed to have become a recluse, spending all his time at his either home or office running the company, which was gradually importing drugs into the kingdom. From his time spent on the dockside, pretending to be a vagrant drunk, Semmental had managed to figure out that Forever came into Haguana's possession through his shipments of imported wines, although this he had not been able to verify on the two occasions he claimed to have been inside the warehouse where the wine was stored. Gremlaw wondered what made Semmental think this was the way Forever was being brought into the kingdom. Semmental in turn told him Haguana now only imported one specific wine, rather than the leathers, silks, spices, other wines, and myriad other items he traded in. Furthermore, the Durana Trading Company had purchased a fleet of flatbed wagons in the past few years to deliver this new product.

Gremlaw spent a fairly comfortable night on an improvised bed made from a pile of scavenged fishing nets covered with a few rough blankets. The rudeness of his surroundings sent his mind back to his earliest recollections of Huleta and the hours they'd spent in the underground hole where she had lived after her mother was killed. Eventually Gremlaw slipped down into the realm of dreams.

The pair rose on the following day, and Gremlaw outlined what he wanted from Semmental, a comprehensive tour of Fitlock Haguana's home and business locations, including any warehouses used for the storage of his wines. He wanted Semmental to act as if he were alone; Gremlaw planned to follow at a distance, as he did not want people to associate the pair.

"How will I know you've seen the places you want to see?" Semmental asked.

"You won't even see me," Gremlaw replied confidently. "Just spend a few minutes leaning against each of the different buildings, and I'll know which ones they are."

Semmental shrugged. "It's your call, my friend. I'll meet you back here later." With that, the emaciated man stooped, shook his hair out into a shaggy mess, and staggered from his hovel.

Gremlaw slipped from the shack a few moments later, after he had scanned the area outside for anything unusual or out of place. Seeing nothing, he disappeared into the first dark space he saw, watching Semmental as he weaved his way, as if drunk, toward one of Haguana's buildings. Gremlaw followed at a distance, always hidden from view. Sometimes he was forced to scale the side of a building and creep across its roof to avoid being seen. Peeking around a corner, Gremlaw noted Semmental pretending to sup from a dirty bottle with his back leaning against a house. From the look of the place, the upkeep had been neglected for some time, as the clapboards across the front had loosened, and the roof sagged. Eventually a pair of brutish-looking men from the local watch came across Semmental and, with many shoves, kicks, and punches, moved him on. Gremlaw dropped silently into the backyard of the house opposite Haguana's and followed Semmental again.

Bottle in hand, Semmental staggered around the town from Haguana's home to his office and from there to the warehouse where the wine and, supposedly, Forever were being kept. Gremlaw made a map of the locations in his mind, scouting the areas surrounding the buildings even as Semmental tottered off toward whatever other destination he had in mind. Finally, the young man settled himself in a hiding spot between some rotting crates and the side of the building opposite Haguana's office. Located close to the Silverdane's waterfront, it could easily be reached by any of the ship captains Haguana had in his employ. Gremlaw's patience eventually paid off just as the sun was setting. Fitlock Haguana made his exit, spending a great deal of time and effort in securing the heavy door. Haguana turned, looked up and down the street, and shuffled off toward his home with Gremlaw in tow not far behind.

The young man spent the next three days shadowing Haguana while questioning Semmental for any information he had gathered on the man and his organization. With all this information in his mind, Gremlaw formulated a plan and rose early the following day to begin its execution. Making sure he had all his meager possessions, he headed for Haguana's office, cloaked in darkness two hours before dawn.

Eerie silence made the streets of Silverdane seem as if they had jumped from the pages of one of the fairy tales Gremlaw's mother had read to him as a child. Mist rolling in from the sea added to the sense of otherworldliness, although Gremlaw welcomed it, slipping through its damp embrace like a shadow. The youth skirted around Haguana's office—he had no chance getting in through the front door anyway—and arrived at the rear of the building. He took a short run up and jumped, using his momentum to gain even more height up the building by using his feet against the vertical surface. Stretching out fully in midair, Gremlaw managed to hook his fingers around a board just below the eaves of the roof. If any part of his entry plan would fail, it was this. He had noted the loose board during one of the trips he had made around

Haguana's properties but hadn't had the opportunity to test whether it would take his weight.

As Gremlaw's weight settled on the edge of the board, he brought his knees up so that he hung just below the edge of the roof. The nails holding the board in place had rusted due to the salty sea air, and several of them broke, dropping Gremlaw a few inches and making him flinch. A squealing sound alerted him that the remaining nails would not hold his weight much longer. He pushed forward and up with his knees, managing to wrap his hands around an upright beam that formed the structure of the building. The length of board he had been hanging from gave way with this added pressure, and Gremlaw only just managed to catch it before it fell. He was counting on the fact that no one would look up and see the missing board, but if it were lying on the ground, it surely would be noticed.

Gremlaw pulled himself up and into the narrow space where the board had been, painfully scraping his back and ribs due to the lack of space. The blackness inside was total, and he had to rely on his other keen senses, which enabled him to locate a crossbeam he could sit on. The young man paused to catch his breath; free climbing into the roof space of the building while grappling with a long piece of wood took a toll even on his athletic body. He managed to wedge the board somewhere near the hole it had come from; no way would it pass a comprehensive examination, but a cursory glance might overlook the hole. Gremlaw then settled in to wait for Fitlock Haguana.

During the next two hours, the morning sun rose in the sky, finding the gaps and holes in the building and providing just enough light for Gremlaw to see the basic layout of the interior. Five or six feet below him sat a large green-leather-topped desk with a few documents on top. Next to this and facing the door sat a once luxurious padded chair; Gremlaw clearly saw the imprint left by Haguana, even in this poor light. One wall was taken up completely with pigeonholes, each holding some kind of document or scroll. On either side of the door, heavy shutters were drawn across the windows and held closed with crossbeams. A vast chest made from highly polished, nearly black wood lay behind Haguana's chair, and a worn, faded rug covered some of the floor.

Gremlaw perched in the darkness of the small office's roof beams for what seemed ages before he heard the clank and squeal of keys turning in massive locks. Moments later, Fitlock Haguana entered his office and threw open the shutters, flooding the area with light. He made his way around his desk, removed his cloak, and placed it gently in the chest Gremlaw had seen. This seemed to be his best chance at surprising the man, so as Haguana turned and seated himself in the chair, which had molded to the contours of his body, Gremlaw lithely lowered himself onto the desk. He landed almost silently and dropped into a squat facing Haguana as the man looked up in shocked amazement.

"'Morning!" Gremlaw announced in a loud voice. The overall effect this had on the man was more than Gremlaw could have wished.

Fitlock Haguana was as pale from shock as Gremlaw had ever seen anyone. His hands and face visibly shook, and his breathing was erratic as his mind struggled to process what he was seeing. He had nut-brown eyes, which were wide at the moment, and his graying hair was pulled back into a ponytail. For a fairly young man, he looked haggard, Gremlaw thought, with sunken cheeks as well as bags under his eyes, as if he had lost a significant amount of weight recently. The idea crossed Gremlaw's mind that he was using the very same narcotic DeLarouge had accused the man of bringing into the kingdom, yet he dismissed this as DeLarouge had said the drug left people vacant and impassive. Haguana wore dark-blue velvet trousers with a white shirt and vest that matched them. One hand displayed a large yet unadorned gold ring, and a silver chain around his neck seemed much more feminine than a man should wear—perhaps a reminder of his wife and daughters, Gremlaw thought.

If Haguana had been caught off guard initially, it was Gremlaw who felt surprise as the man slapped his thigh and chuckled only a few heartbeats after seeing him perched on his desk. Gremlaw tilted his head and waited.

"I do apologize," Haguana eventually managed, "however, the smith I engaged to install the locks and bars ensured me none may gain entry, and here we are, less than a month later, and you have circumnavigated the system! Astounding! I should have words with the man, if it even mattered." Haguana's jovial tone turned sour at the end of his speech.

"I didn't come in through the front," Gremlaw told him, "so your investment was a good one."

Nodding, Haguana pulled open a drawer and reached for something inside. He stopped as soon as he noticed Gremlaw's hand dart beneath his cloak. "I have no weaponry concealed, I assure you," the merchant said. "Just a few tipples of a fine vintage and a glass or two. Would you mind?"

"Slow," Gremlaw cautioned.

True to his word, Haguana brought out a bottle and two glasses and poured a drink for both of them. He took his glass and drained the contents in one gulp, refilling the glass immediately. Haguana looked up into Gremlaw's eyes and raised an eyebrow. "So a Trathlainian, eh? I thought my life would be terminated by someone from, shall we say, another land."

"I'm not a killer. I'm a thief," Gremlaw stated calmly.

"Well, that is easily solved then!" Haguana declared. "I have very little here. However, I have a vault at my home that contains vast sums for an enterprising young man such as yourself."

The sarcasm was not lost on Gremlaw, who felt his anger rise. "I'm sure you do have vast sums stashed in that house of yours, Haguana, especially as you're importing and distributing poisonous drugs into the border garrisons!" The young man dropped from the desk and stood opposite Haguana. "So you thought Lavashians would come and kill you. Why?"

Haguana paled once more, and his hands shook as he poured another drink. It took several moments for him to answer. "M-my warehouse.

Someone has entered the warehouse and tampered with the deliveries that contain…that must contain…you know…" He trailed off, as if unable to say the word.

"Forever?" Gremlaw supplied, and Haguana nodded. "We couldn't find anything with the wines, couldn't find the drug."

Haguana's eyes widened, and he pointed an accusatory finger at Gremlaw. "You!" he cried. "It was you who broke in and rifled through the shipment!"

Gremlaw shook his head. "Not me. Someone I know. If it had been me, you wouldn't have even known I'd been here. How do they do it, Haguana? How do they get the drug into the kingdom so easily?"

Haguana wiped a hand across his sweating brow. "Curse me. I know not!" he shouted. "I have personally examined each bottle in several of the shipments brought in and can find nothing amiss. Yet the fact remains that it all adds up—every indicator leads back here—and I knew it would be only a matter of time before someone like you turned up." He grunted a derisive laugh. "I suppose I should be thankful I'm not being dragged away in irons."

Gremlaw nodded. "Not yet at least," he said, "but treason has quite a high price."

Haguana dropped his glass onto the desk and leaned back in his chair. "They kidnapped my wife and daughters, you know," he said in a voice thick with emotion, "took them in the dead of night and said they would be tortured and killed if I didn't agree to do everything they wished. Little Della is not yet fifteen, and Matra is probably the same age as you." Haguana's shoulders shook as he sobbed over the loss of his family.

Gremlaw felt a lump form in his throat; this poor soul was in a similar situation to himself, and he knew how difficult that was to bear. Images of his mother and Huleta flashed through his mind as he stood and tried to formulate a response. "Believe it or not," he began, "I know what you're going through." Haguana looked up at him in disbelief. "And how hard it is to do what's best." Gremlaw took a deep breath and released it before gently asking, "How do you know they're even still alive?"

Haguana turned and opened the chest behind him. He pulled out a packet of letters and threw it on top of the green leather of his desk. "Each time a wine shipment is delivered, I receive one letter from my wife or one of my daughters, detailing how they're being treated and looked after." He fixed Gremlaw with a hope-filled expression. "This proves they're safe, does it not?"

Gremlaw smiled and nodded, not mentioning he knew of people in the capital who were able to re-create handwriting styles and tones of writing and even used special inks and papers along with perfectly carved stamps and seals.

"So the Lavashians have you under their control," Gremlaw stated quietly.

Haguana dropped his head in shame, and the pair fell silent. If Gremlaw could not gain any information from him, he would have to travel to one of the garrison towns and attempt to trace the trail there.

"There are two ways this can go for now," Gremlaw said in no uncertain terms. "Either I report back to the man I work for, and he sends a force of men to seize you and all your assets, which of course means you and your family will die…" Haguana's tortured face pulled at Gremlaw, yet he had to do this in order to save his own loved ones. "Or," he continued, "you can add me as a guard to one of your new wagons and let me see where this trail ends."

Haguana slumped down once more, a sense of relief clearly washing through him. "Thank you!" he said over and over. "Thank you!"

Gremlaw shook his head. "Haguana, this will catch up to you eventually, and when it does, your life will be forfeited. The kingdom cannot allow you to get away with this, and the Lavashians…" He paused for a moment. "Well, you know more about them than I do." Haguana took his meaning immediately. "Give yourself up, plead to the mercy of the crown, tell them all you know, and you might be allowed your life."

Haguana laughed bitterly. "A life of hard labor in the mines?" he said sarcastically. "I don't believe I'm suited for such hardships, do you? No, of course you don't. Since they took my girls…" His voice caught as he mentioned his wife and daughters. "In the absence of my family, I have come to realize there is a pointlessness to life. If it ends with a rope around my neck, so be it."

Gremlaw looked upon him with a dispassionate expression he did not feel inside and asked, "When is the next delivery due to leave?"

CHAPTER 7

Gremlaw rocked from side to side as the covered wagon he rode in swayed along the rutted roads of the kingdom of Trathlain. He had forced Haguana into allowing him to join one of the teams responsible for the distribution of the wine—which somehow held the secret of Forever—within the kingdom. Horrible guilt crawled through him as he recalled his meeting with the owner of the Durana Trading Company. Could he have done more to persuade the man to try to save his own life? Although, Gremlaw thought, even if he had, what kind of life would it be? Haguana was in a dire situation, with few easy options, and even though Gremlaw had not been responsible for any of it, he felt a deep sadness for the man.

"You's quiet today, m'boy!" Jornsa observed in his colloquial manner. An old man, Jornsa was the uneducated son of an uneducated father and had run away to sea at age thirteen to save his family the expense of keeping him and his siblings. His easy manner and gentle kindliness reminded Gremlaw of his father, and the pair had become friends almost immediately. Although Gremlaw had to fashion a story regarding his background, he kept as much truth to the tale as he could, simply stating that his family and Haguana's were linked by marriage and that he had asked for some work.

"He be a good man, that Fitlock Haguana," Jornsa had declared after Gremlaw had told him this. "Many's a man who'da cast me aside after I been havin' my accident." Jornsa had fallen from the rigging of one of Haguana's ships, breaking an arm, leg, and several of his fingers. Haguana had seen to it that he had medical attention and paid him a small sum for his wife and sons to live on while he recuperated. Once Jornsa had healed, Haguana had given him charge of a pair of horses and a wagon and sent him all over this part of the world to make deliveries.

"What ails you, m'boy?" Jornsa asked.

Gremlaw smiled, "Just thinking, old man. Just thinking."

Jornsa made a crude noise and added his wisdom to the conversation. "There ain't be nothin' a lad of yourn age needs to be thinkin' 'bout 'cept where he goin' ta get the next drink, next meal, or next bit o' flesh!"

Gremlaw laughed. "I have a girl back home," he said, wondering if he indeed did.

"Yar," Jornsa said wisely, "but she's not 'ere now, is she? And it ain't like you's married. What's the harm in gettin' a bit o' comp'ny while you's away?"

Gremlaw shook his head. This debate had been going on for most of the five-day journey, and he still could not get the aging teamster to see his point of view. The young man fell back on a previous argument. "So will *you* be looking out for some female companionship in town then?"

Jornsa looked at Gremlaw as if he had asked him to eat live puppies. "God's teeth, boy!" Jornsa swore. "I be's a married man!" A smile cut through his look of false horror.

"And you take your wedding vows seriously?" Gremlaw asked.

"'Course I do, boy!" Jornsa scratched the side of his bearded cheek. "That, and if the wife found out I'd been puttin' it about, she'd more'n likely cut off me tallywacker with a rusty kitchen knife." The old man guffawed loudly as Gremlaw chuckled.

"That's a picture I'll struggle to get out of my head!" Gremlaw said, making Jornsa laugh harder.

The horses whinnied as the outfit rounded a corner at the base of a hill, revealing a town with high gray walls, pennons and flags bearing the royal crest of Trathlain, and a greasy pall of black smoke that hung over the town like a headache.

"Look lively, m'boy. We's almost there!"

Gremlaw gazed toward the depressed town of Strathnave and realized this was the reality of living in a border garrison town; the civilian populace here existed only to provide food and supplies for the soldiers who manned the fort. As the pair approached the town, Gremlaw noted the gates hung partially open, and there were no guards on top of the walls or on sentry duty at the gate. As the wagon passed into town unchecked, a feeling of dread grew inside Gremlaw; something was badly wrong here. No doubt the garrison would be spotless, yet the level of decay, filth, and general disrepair that marked the civilian section was horrific to witness. No sooner had the wagon passed through the unmanned gates than Gremlaw saw piles of rubbish along the bases of walls and the remains of burned buildings smoldering in the gray light beneath the layer of smoke that hung over the town.

Gremlaw looked at his companion with an expression of disgust. Jornsa pursed his lips and said, "Used to be this here Strathnave were a nice little town. Then war comed, and people, they don' get the point of lookin' after a place what might be run over by them Lavashians any day."

This brutal statement summed up the essence of the whole town, and Gremlaw's heart sank as he considered the ramifications.

The wagon trundled through the dirty streets, empty of human traffic save for the odd fleeting glimpse of a shadow disappearing around a corner. Gremlaw saw more devastation with every clop of the horses' hooves than he'd seen in his life. It seemed as if the entire infrastructure of Strathnave had fallen apart, and no one bothered to maintain his property. One or two of the stone structures even had collapsed due to the heat from uncontrolled fires in adjacent buildings. Briefly wondering whether the buildings' inhabitants were still inside, Gremlaw suppressed a shudder.

As Jornsa steered his wagon toward a large warehouse as far from the military outpost as possible, he turned and quietly said, "'Tis a nasty bit o' work what runs this warehouse, m'boy, burn-faced man by the name of Reloen. Keep your eyes an' ears open, m'boy. But don' be lookin' round too much. There be things here you ain't want to see." Although Gremlaw thought the exact opposite, he understood the driver's meaning.

Jornsa halted the wagon outside the large warehouse, which was well looked after in comparison to the rest of the town, and got down to hammer on the doors. The man who opened the doors to allow the wagon entry stomped toward them after closing them once Jornsa had pulled the wagon inside. Gremlaw nearly recoiled as he saw that half the man's head had been horribly burned. His left eye had been burned out completely, and the waxy, yellow scar tissue that covered half his head sported no hair.

"Jornsa," he growled, "got me bottles?" The driver nodded curtly, so the disfigured man ordered, "Drop 'em over by yonder door." He pointed to a smaller building inside the main warehouse. Gremlaw began to untie the sheet that had been thrown across the cargo, and Jornsa dragged one of the crates across and placed it next to the door Reloen had indicated.

"Got yerself a new sword arm, Jornsa?" Reloen growled sarcastically while gesturing toward Gremlaw, who was pretending to bungle his way through the operation. Reloen pulled a small flask from inside his leather coat and sipped from it. Immediately Gremlaw wondered whether he was using Forever, yet if DeLarouge were correct, he seemed far too lucid.

Halfway through the unloading process, Gremlaw smelled the pungent odor of what seemed to be burning fruit coming from within the smaller building and wondered what it was. "Sir," he addressed the burned man, "I be thinking you's got a fire inside, sir." His natural mimicry of a peasant boy was flawless.

"Don't be worryin' yer pretty little head about that, m'boy. 'Tis nothing."

As soon as the scarred man said this, the door in the smaller building was wrenched open. The dim light inside the wooden room revealed two odd-looking men, and Gremlaw instantly wondered whether these were Lavashians blatantly working inside the kingdom. After one glance at their massive, round eyes, which reflected even the low light in the warehouse, the memories Mishu somehow had transferred to him leaped to the front of his mind, confirming his suspicion. Glancing beyond them, Gremlaw saw the room was an array of copper piping and tubes he associated with apothecary use. This then was the source of the smell; they were boiling the wine for some reason.

Gremlaw's puzzled mind tried to sort through this new information when Jornsa screamed, "Lavashians!" Before staring dumbly down at the foot-long, bloodied sword blade that had punched through his chest, the old man glanced pleadingly at Gremlaw. A fountain of blood sprayed from his mouth, and he collapsed to his knees then slumped forward off Reloen's sword.

Panic rose in Gremlaw's chest as the scarred man turned toward him. The two Lavashians were systematically smashing their chemists' equipment to pieces, and one took a hammer to the newly delivered bottles. He sent a nasty look in Gremlaw's direction as he let the wine flow onto the packed dirt of the floor.

As fear poured adrenaline into his bloodstream, Gremlaw felt his consciousness shift, allowing him to see negative space, yet he could see no viable means of escape, as even half blind, the scarred man was viper fast. Reloen quickly closed in on Gremlaw, who drew his long dagger from beneath his cloak in an attempt to defend himself.

Reloen's burned face shifted into a gruesome parody of a grin, and his voice rang out, echoing in the warehouse. "I'll gut you, boy!" he growled as Gremlaw tried to back away.

Gremlaw felt his consciousness shift again, and time seemed to slow as it had with Dron in training. He saw Reloen's muscles tense in preparation to stab him and noticed his remaining eye fix just below his own ribcage. Gremlaw dropped to one knee and leaned into Reloen's blind spot while bracing his dagger for an upward thrust. As Reloen's sword thrust narrowly missed Gremlaw's shoulder, burying the point into the wall, the young man drove his dagger up through the scarred man's belly and into his chest. Gremlaw stared as Reloen's single eye widened with the pain and shock of the stab. Lifting the blade with as much force as he could manage, the youth sliced it into his opponent's intestines before sliding into his right lung and skimming his heart just deep enough to cut into one of the ventricles.

Gremlaw watched as the life faded from Reloen's single eye, and his knees buckled, pitching the man forward onto Gremlaw. The young man twisted himself sideways and scrambled from beneath Reloen's corpse.

Faintly Gremlaw became aware of someone repeatedly saying, "I'm sorry. I'm sorry." It took the youth nearly a full minute to realize it was himself. Abruptly he turned and retched onto the warehouse floor, the muscles in his body straining as if to expunge the image of the dead man and his own guilt over what he had done. He had murdered someone! Immediately visions of watch soldiers appeared in his mind, swarming into the warehouse and taking him into custody.

Unable to wrench his gaze away from the man's single, astounded eye, Gremlaw pulled his blade from the body of the man he had just killed. Wide with shock and fear, the single orb would haunt Gremlaw's nightmares for years. He sprinted past the array of alchemy supplies without really noticing any of it as he heedlessly plunged onward. The room was fairly short and narrow, more of a corridor, Gremlaw thought, as he rushed toward the gaping maw of a doorway through which he assumed the two men had left. Pausing and holding his breath, he regained enough of his sensibilities to listen for any possible assailants outside.

Deciding no ambush was waiting for him beyond the door, Gremlaw stepped into a rubbish-strewn alleyway. To his left, the alley ran along the rear of the warehouse and ended in what looked to be a solid wall. To his right, it continued toward an open area, and Gremlaw's quick eyes noticed a flap of dark material catch briefly on the rough edge of the warehouse before being pulled around the corner. He darted forth in pursuit of the two Lavashians.

At the end of the alleyway, Gremlaw peered around to see two black-robed figures running along the street. Although a few people were staggering along here, no one took any notice of the fleeing men. Gremlaw took off after them as fast as his rubbery legs would carry him. As they ventured deeper into the heart of the town, the foot traffic picked up somewhat, and a few heads turned as the Lavashian agents roughly shoved their way through the milling people. Whether it was due to the horror Gremlaw felt at his act of murder or some other unknown reason, his vision refused to show negative space; no green outlines appeared, and no subsequent tunnels could be seen. Gremlaw was as disadvantaged as the Lavashians when it came to threading his way through the people here.

Eventually he came to an open marketplace, if it could be called such. Molded together in the center, like prisoners huddled in a cell, a group of traders bravely had set up and were valiantly trying to peddle their wares, all to no avail. Gremlaw stopped to scan the square, looking for the two men he sought and noticing a commotion on the far side of the square. The two fleeing men were trying to bull their way through a bunched crowd of slack-jawed, vacant-eyed men and women. In turn, the people of this desperate town were grabbing for the two men and moaning as if their very lives depended on the pair. Utterly confused, Gremlaw skirted the periphery of the marketplace, passing rundown homes and closed businesses. Nearing the boiling mass of humanity that still held the two men he was chasing, he saw a flash of steel and a spray of blood as the two Lavashians butchered their way out of the crowd. Gremlaw felt his gorge rise again while he witnessed this slaughter of men and women alike. He could not understand what force drove the populace of the town to behave like this; as one person was brutally murdered, another reached for the men. Eventually their swords won out, and the two Lavashians raced off in the direction they had been traveling.

Gremlaw could not have given chase even if he had felt the urge to. He felt as if his bones had been removed from inside his legs, and he slid to the ground with his back against the wall of a partially burned house. Even if he caught up with the pair, what could he hope to do? Gremlaw never had been much of a fighter, and the techniques Dron had taught him were more for self-defense and to assist his natural ability to escape and evade. His witnessing of the slaughter here convinced him he was not able to fight these men.

More disturbing than the actual slaughter was the residents' reaction to it, as no one seemed interested in helping the dying or clearing the dead. Gremlaw's sense of dread upon entering this town had been justified. Something was horrendously wrong with these people; he just did not know what.

Gremlaw took a deep breath and stayed seated with his back to the wall when it hit him again. He had killed someone!

He leaned forward, held his head in his hands, and dropped the long dagger he had used to murder Reloen. A violent trembling shook his thin body, making his teeth chatter, a result of the adrenaline withdrawing from his system and the shock he felt at the admission he had made to himself.

A dichotomy of consciousness existed within Gremlaw's mind; one personality was horrified at the act he had committed, while the other remained much more rational.

I knew I was a thief, but a killer? the first Gremlaw thought.

He would have killed me! It was self-defense, came the thought of the second.

I'm a murderer!

No, you're alive! his other self stated firmly. *He would have killed you!*

Still he might have had a family, friends who'll miss him.

He stabbed Jornsa through the back and was helping those two Lavashians do whatever it was they were doing.

But his face—I can still see his face.

On this point, the second voice in his mind was perfectly silent. Tears dripped down Gremlaw's cheeks, partially dissolving the blood that caked his hands.

The pointless conversation rolled over and over inside his head until he thought he would go mad. He groped for the blade he had dropped, noticing the rust-brown stains of dried blood on his hand as he did. Painful guilt slammed into Gremlaw as he retched. Not one of the vacant-eyed passersby paid any attention to the blood-spattered youth who was violently heaving bile onto the ground. Gremlaw squatted in his own vomit until the trembling feelings passed. He stood, muscles aching as if he were a hundred years old, and stumbled off toward...where? Gremlaw had no idea what to do or where to go.

CHAPTER 8

Sitting on a bench, Gremlaw considered his options as sunlight filtered through the branches of a tree and onto his back. He thought he should make his way back to warn Fitlock Haguana that the Lavashians were probably aware he had been compromised. Then he wondered whether he should have Semmental send word to DeLarouge but dismissed the idea, as it would take too much time. Gremlaw looked around him, assessing the grubby little outpost for a possible solution.

Something nagged at the back of his mind, vying for attention with his guilt over killing of the one-eyed man. Closing his eyes, he tried to force the guilt aside so he could concentrate on this new thought. As people shuffled past him on mindless errands, Gremlaw's head shot up as he realized what his mind already had registered. There was virtually no sound! No raised voices, with the exception of the few vendors in the marketplace. No screaming children howling at the unfairness of being dragged around the market—in fact, he could see no children at all. He watched an old woman stumble past where he sat; her vacant, open-mouthed expression made his flesh crawl almost as much as the emptiness in her eyes. Gremlaw looked at a younger man whose face conveyed the same emptiness. Almost everyone he saw appeared to be in the same state of mind. Blank faces greeted him wherever he glanced, and the terrifying probability of the situation crossed his mind.

If Lavashian agents had managed to spread Forever throughout the populace here—and worse, the military outpost—they would have a gateway into the kingdom of Trathlain. Those two Lavashians had been boiling the wine at the warehouse, feeding it through tubes, and collecting some liquid from the other end. Somehow that must be how they processed Forever. It was in *every* bottle of wine, not just the occasional bottle in each shipment, as Haguana initially had thought. As a plan formed in his mind, Gremlaw stood and made his way back to the marketplace.

At a public fountain with a filthy pool of stagnant water in the base, he scrubbed the encrusted blood from his hands, trying to think of anything but the single wide eye of Reloen. Once he finished, he headed toward the few traders who had been outgoing enough to set up their stalls yet were now taking them back down and packing their wares away unsold. Gremlaw walked past the short row of stalls a few times, listening to them talk among themselves as they packed their goods onto carts. The youth noticed two of them shared a larger wagon and wondered whether they had formed a partnership.

"We needs to get away from 'ere, Dorrian," one said as he lifted bundles of cloth into the back of the wagon. "There's somethin' real bad happ'nin' in this town."

"Ye won't be getting any arguing from me, Nims," Dorrian replied. "I don't be knowin' nothin' 'bout what be wrong, but me old dad used to tell ghost stories to us young'uns what sounded exactly like this looks." He threw one hand around to indicate the whole town.

Gremlaw made his choice while he listened. This pair was probably his best, if not only, chance to get a message to DeLarouge, and he made his approach quite noisily. "You men, listen up." The two men turned, shocked at the sound of his voice. "I'll tell you what has happened here if you do me and your kingdom a great service."

Dorrian and Nims took in Gremlaw's disheveled, bloodstained clothing and were instantly frightened. "Don't ye be comin' no closer!" Dorrian warned as he reached for the hilt of a dagger at his belt. "We don't be holdin' with no ghostly people," he added, which made Gremlaw smile.

"You have nothing to fear from me, good sirs," Gremlaw reassured. "I just need to get a message to the capital, more precisely to Duke Wattiern DeLarouge."

"Go on," Nims said cautiously.

Gremlaw told the pair of merchants about some of the things he had discovered and made sure they knew how important it was for them to leave as soon as possible.

"Ain't be gettin' no argument from me," Nims told Gremlaw, "quite 'appy I'll be to see civilized people again."

The young man made sure both traders repeated the message he wanted to get to DeLarouge before wishing them a safe journey. Gremlaw knew it would take a few weeks for the pair to get the message to the capital in person, yet he had no idea if all the garrison towns had been poisoned off in this way and could not risk his message being intercepted.

Gremlaw needed to get away from Strathnave and its Lavashian influences before he was introduced to Forever a little too closely. The young man kept to the shadows as much as he could while making his way toward the gate through which Jornsa had delivered him. *Could that really have been earlier today?* Gremlaw wondered. So much had happened since he had killed the one-eyed man that it felt as though half a lifetime had passed. His guilt came flooding back, and his normal early-warning systems of vision and hearing failed abysmally to alert him to the presence of a group of people hidden in deep shadows that had stationed itself in the mouth of an alley.

Gremlaw nearly stumbled into one of the hooded characters, whose face was almost completely hidden beneath a thick, hooded cloak.

"Stupid, look out!" the man said in a thickly accented voice. Something familiar pulled at Gremlaw's attention, and he realized he had heard this accent only once before, coming from the lips of Dron's wife, Mishu, a defector from the empire of Lavash.

"Sorry," Gremlaw mumbled, attempting to become as vacantly empty-headed as the rest of Strathnave's population. Unfortunately for him, this was completely the wrong thing to do, as the small group of Lavashians started the trading process.

"Paying us for Forever...How will you?" the Lavashian whom Gremlaw almost had knocked into asked in his mangled Trathlainian. He apparently had mistaken Gremlaw for one of the locals who had come looking for their next fix, and the young man had no desire to become hooked on this pernicious drug. Shaking his head, Gremlaw took a few steps backward, away from the group of men, who had all turned to face him. Whatever the pair of men at the rear of the group had been doing, they obviously had finished, as they faced him too. Gremlaw could not understand why his legs buckled beneath him, and he fell to his knees on the grimy pavement. As the stunning pain, which began to spread across the back of his skull, crept around to steal his vision, the last sight he registered was of a young woman. A look of abject terror was plastered across her young face as she struggled to walk away from the group. As fingers of white fog misted across Gremlaw's eyes, her face gradually changed into one that mirrored the rest of the population; slack-jawed and vacant, she became another victim of Forever.

*   *   *

"Zha-Quin will want to see..."

"What are we supposed to..."

"We ought to just kill hi..."

It was the incessant, remorseless thumping that radiated from the back of Gremlaw's head that proved to him that he was still alive. Trying to reach around to feel if his skull had been smashed, he discovered his hands had been tied to something. He allowed his eyes to flicker open and take in the sight of a partially rotten straw roof a few feet above him. A spike of scent rammed into his nostrils: urine and feces combined with damp straw. Glancing to one side, the young man saw his wrists had been chained to a wooden wall on either side of him. All this information pointed to his being kept in a stable, although he had no idea where or by whom.

Trying to ignore the pain from his battered skull, he lifted his head to see a little better.

"Go tell Zha-Quin his little sleeper has awoken," a male voice stated eloquently.

Even though it had been eloquently spoken, Gremlaw realized it had not been said in his mother tongue. This led to the two questions: What language was it, and how had Gremlaw come to know it?

Looking up, he saw a man staring back into his eyes. Small and stocky in appearance, the man had huge, round eyes—half again as large as Gremlaw's—that took over the top half of his face. A small nose and thin-lipped mouth sat below these orbs, which held Gremlaw's attention.

"Wake, wake," the man said in a heavily accented voice that marked him as a Lavashian. "Sleep you be long period."

Gremlaw grunted. "So would you if your skull had been shattered."

The Lavashian laughed harshly. "Sickly boy," he said before turning his attention to someone who had just entered. "Zha-Quin, sir," he spoke in his own tongue while snapping to attention, "your prisoner has awoken."

Gremlaw had no time to puzzle over his ability to understand the Lavashian tongue as a vaguely familiar face entered his vision. It took a few seconds for his concussed brain to make the connection; this was one of the two Lavashian agents who had been processing the wine in the warehouse, the one who had stared directly at Gremlaw. He also was one of the people who had slaughtered innocent men and women in cold blood.

A good foot taller than the other man, Zha-Quin looked down with the same large eyes, a vicious grin spreading across his face as he replied to his subordinate, "Go and seek refreshments, Min Sa. I will summon you later." The shorter man saluted and left quickly. Zha-Quin's doe-like eyes contained no compassion whatsoever as he turned to Gremlaw's prone form. "Manage to cost much money you have. Who are you?"

"Speak in a civilized tongue, or keep your mouth shut!" Gremlaw spat in defiance. His hatred for this man who had poisoned and slaughtered innocent Trathlainians and forced his own hand into killing Reloen incited a rebellious anger within him. Once the words left his mouth, however, Gremlaw yelped in agony as Zha-Quin stomped viciously on his shin, grinding the rough sole of his hobnailed boot into skin and bone.

"Not understanding. You say what?" The Lavashian's huge eyes flashed in a dangerous manner.

Trying to will away the pain, Gremlaw drew in a shuddering breath and spat his answer through gritted teeth. "Is it all men from Lavash or just you whose mother had relationships with cattle?"

Gremlaw was surprised when Zha-Quin grunted a small laugh and actually provided an answer. "My mother just," he replied, removing his foot. Switching to his native language, Zha-Quin called out a number of orders. Gremlaw's understanding of the language led him to realize the Lavashian agents were about to move him. His heart sank as Zha-Quin told one of his men they would be home within a fortnight.

CHAPTER 9

Lavashian travel practices were as alien as the landscape through which Gremlaw was being dragged. Having never set foot outside his home city before this madness had befallen him, the youth was in a state of constant surprise as the small band made their way through the empire of Lavash. While Trathlain was a verdant land filled with forests and grasslands, fields of crops, and herds of cattle, Lavash was a barren wasteland composed of stony soil that barely supported the few scrubby bushes managing to eke out an existence in the harsh environment. The border between the two countries was as stark as the slash of a sword across a throat, morphing from lush green to barren wasteland in the space of half a day's travel. The band of men passed through the craggy hills that separated the two countries after leaving the broken, demoralized border town behind with no challenge or resistance whatsoever.

Zha-Quin led the trio that consisted of him and two similarly dressed Lavashians, all mounted on horseback. They were followed by Min Sa, whom Gremlaw had been guarded by as he woke up after being cudgeled, and another Lavashian, similarly attired to Min Sa, who walked along on Gremlaw's other side. Zha-Quin and his two friends trotted at a leisurely pace, chatting and making jokes as they rode. The two smaller men who flanked Gremlaw were silent as they nudged him along the dusty road that led north, deeper into the empire of Lavash.

Gremlaw's hands were tied together at the wrists and elbows and behind his back, making it extremely difficult to walk, as his balance was askew. He staggered along, the pain from his battered skull and stomped-on leg distracting him from his ruminations. Lavashian society seemed to be split into two castes; Zha-Quin and his pair of lackeys were taller, broader, and more muscular, with darker skin than the two men who were responsible for dragging Gremlaw along. As he listened to the banter that Zha-Quin and his two high-caste peers threw back and forth as they rode, he realized it must have been the painful, confusing exchange of memories he had shared with Dron's wife Mishu that had made it possible for him to understand the Lavashian tongue. Her memories were quiet inside his mind and only seemed to come to the forefront of his consciousness as needed. Gremlaw assumed this was a normal function of his brain, as although he spoke Trathlainian, he could not remember specifically learning the language. It was the same with Mishu's memories; they did not interfere with his thought processes in the least, yet he could recall everything she remembered if he thought about it. Having time to examine this odd phenomenon as he stomped along a Lavashian road, Gremlaw was surprised he had not been changed by the whole ordeal. If the events of his life had shaped who he was, as some said, then would the addition of another complete personality into his brain eventually change his perspective to include the experiences of this other personality? It was a worrying thought to Gremlaw. Would he become more feminine? Fall in love with a man? The possibilities were a little daunting; would the other personality take over some of the time? Or would a gradual blending of his and Mishu's personalities take effect? Gremlaw had no clue. He was, however, aware of how weird it felt to remember giving birth to a child.

Reaching what once appeared to have been a fairly large village as the sun began to set, Zha-Quin ordered the two lower-caste men to make sure Gremlaw was securely tied before they scurried around to find firewood and set a few animal traps. Apparently, these lower-caste members were either servants or slaves to the higher-ranking men who seemed to do nothing but idly stand and chat. They placed Gremlaw at the corner of a derelict house and lowered him almost carefully onto a pile of dry leaves that the wind had gathered. As with the few other structures he had seen in this land, Gremlaw noted they had been built from sandstone blocks, probably the reason for their continued existence. Any wood or cloth had long since decayed, leaving the footprints of the buildings in the middle of this vast, empty expanse.

Min Sa brought a bowl of weak soup over and wordlessly made sure Gremlaw drank the whole thing before grunting, "Sleep."

A weak sun was slowly born into the sky, sending pale fingers of light crawling through the rundown structures and uncovering the shivering form of Gremlaw, still bound in a corner. Barely able to think due to the paralyzing chill, the young man could not feel his fingers, and pain had blossomed in his shoulders and between his shoulder blades due to the tight bonds that held him. The rough hands of Min Sa and his equal pulled Gremlaw to his feet, but there was no way his legs were capable of obeying his commands, and he stumbled, falling to his knees, then his chest and face. Gremlaw became aware of the intensity of pain as the men untied his arms; he felt a singularly unpleasant pulling sensation *within* his flesh as the ties were loosened. Coupled with the pulling came sharp stinging stabs from his elbows all the way down to his fingers. This was the worst; his fingertips were so incredibly sensitive that it was agonizing to accidentally brush them across his clothing.

Gritting his teeth against the forceful pain, Gremlaw tried not to cry out, but the severity of pain, like knives being driven through his muscles, made him groan, especially upon moving his shoulders. His stinging hands were brought before him, making him gasp, and retied in front of his body. As an added precaution, he was tethered to the saddle of Zha-Quin's horse and dragged along the road. Eventually Gremlaw became unable to keep pace with the horse and fell, the wrenching agony in his shoulders almost enough to make him pass out but not quite. Either not noticing or, more likely, not caring, Zha-Quin allowed Gremlaw to be dragged along the rough surface of the road as slivers of sharp rocks slashed his flesh and ripped his clothes. Valiantly Gremlaw tried to regain his feet but ended up stumbling once more. This time his consciousness fled.

*　*　*

From the familiar sounds of the heavy bolts being dragged from the far side of the door, Jocinta Haguana knew she and her two daughters would soon receive a visit from one of the barbarians who held them captive. For more than three months, she and her children had been subjected to imprisonment in this savage land. They had no rights and no privacy; some of the men even had come in to watch the trio use the bucket that served as a toilet. The food, if it could be called such, was the plainest fare she'd ever tasted, and she had been a sailor's daughter before her marriage to her dear Fitlock. These savages—as she could refer to them as nothing else—fed them a staple diet of beans, bread, and water. All three had lost a great deal of weight; little Della's ribs plainly could be seen through the gaping hole in her dress.

Jocinta's two daughters yelped screams of fright as the savage Lavashians roughly shoved what appeared to be a person into the prison with them. As Jocinta regarded the slim youth who had been dumped into the small room, a protective instinct took over. "Matra! Della!" she barked at her cowering daughters. "Help me get him into my bed!" The girls remained where they were and simply stared, wide-eyed, at the body bleeding on the floor. Jocinta shook her head. "Look, dears," she told them calmly, "I know this man has been badly hurt, but look at his face, see past his injuries, and truly see his features." She watched as her daughters looked, before adding, "He's from Trathlain. He's a fellow countryman and in need of our help."

Matra and Della edged toward Gremlaw's injured body as if approaching a dangerous animal rather than an unconscious youth, doing as their mother instructed and looking down on him with apprehensive compassion. The sisters looked at each other in surprise before glancing at their mother and nodding. Even with the three females working together, and taking into consideration Gremlaw's thin frame, it was a battle of epic proportions to get him onto Jocinta's low pallet. Once Jocinta had caught her breath, she took a cloth she had ripped from her dress and dipped it in the small supply of water they had been allowed. Then she gently dabbed at the hundreds of scratches he had sustained, bringing him back to the world of the living. She set her daughters to ripping strips from their own clothes to use as bandages on the deeper cuts, which still bled, while she cleaned the dust from around his young eyes.

"He's barely yet a man," Jocinta observed as the layers of dirt gave their secrets up.

"Will he survive, Mother?" Della asked in her now always subdued voice.

Jocinta's heart broke again as she heard the desolation in her youngest daughter's voice. Della had been the one who had kept up her spirits the longest—all the way from the darkness of the stinking ship where they had been held in darkness, through the short cart ride that had brought them to this desolate outpost, and even during the first few weeks of incarceration. Della's imprisonment eventually had taken its toll on her, however, and she had withdrawn into herself, stopped spouting her hopeful statements about how her father would sort it all out.

"Only time will tell, my love," Jocinta answered her. "If infection sets in, he's probably done for."

Gremlaw's mind swam in a sea of pain. His very brain seemed to throb, and he felt as if something were standing on his nose. He also felt as if someone had dragged him across a graveled surface for three or four weeks, as the skin from his chest and upper arms sent messages of flaming agony to his brain. He groaned weakly and felt a soothing coolness across his forehead. Gremlaw allowed his eyes to flutter open for a second to focus on a kind-looking female face before he descended into darkness once more.

He woke sometime later, a low groan of pain escaping his cracked lips as he became fully conscious. Gremlaw looked down to see his naked chest had been bandaged, and dressings had been applied to his upper arms. His eyes focused on two girls and one older woman, who had all turned at his exclamation. The two girls blushed at his semi-dressed condition, as he had thrown off the light blanket that had covered him. The older of the three made her graceful way toward him as his quick mind discerned something familiar in the faces of the two girls.

"Greetings, sir," the woman said. "Do you understand me?"

Gremlaw nodded. "Where am I?" he asked, his dry throat making his voice sound strange even to himself.

The woman dipped her head to one side and sadly replied, "We're all prisoners somewhere in this godforsaken land. You've been unconscious for nearly a week and not said anything. Might we know your name?"

"Gremlaw," he replied in a rasp as the connections fit together in his brain. He allowed his painful lips to form a smile as he said, "I didn't believe Fitlock when he said you three were still alive." The young man reveled in the surprised expressions that crossed the faces of the Haguana ladies. "But he was right."

*　*　*

Duke Wattiern DeLarouge paced the length of the stone-walled room where he waited for the most powerful man in the kingdom to summon him. Even this antechamber dripped with opulence, as it was decorated with portraits and statues of the royal family from years gone by and possessed rich woolen tapestries that draped down the walls like silk garments over the curves of a woman. Even DeLarouge, used to fine living and expensive surroundings, found this excess overwhelming as he dodged plush-cushioned and gilt sofas. A door opened, and DeLarouge watched as the queen seemed to float past his position, nodding gracefully to him as he bowed low before her. She laid a single finger on his shoulder, as light as a butterfly landing, and told him, "You may enter now." The queen breathed deeply as she sauntered across the room.

"Majesty," DeLarouge responded. He rose and strode to the wooden portal through which he found His Majesty, King Garnandius, staring at the city below him. DeLarouge took three steps toward his king and dropped to one knee, offering the back of his neck in the traditional genuflection.

Garnandius turned slightly before returning his attention to his capital. "Get up, Wattiern." His deep voice reverberated around the cavernous chamber. "You know there is no need to kneel when it is just you and me." He turned as DeLarouge rose again. "Now what is this dire information you have come across?" DeLarouge watched as the king seated himself in a vast chair and gestured for the duke to sit as well.

"A pair of traders in cheap goods nearly killed their horses to deliver a message from someone I sent to infiltrate the Durana Trading Company, sire," DeLarouge started. Garnandius nodded his understanding, so the duke continued. "They said an old friend of mine wanted me to get a message to his mother." DeLarouge's guilty eyes flashed to the impassive face of his king. "I was supposed to let her know Strathnave has been lost to Forever."

Garnandius' eyebrows rose as he recognized the name of the border outpost. "Strathnave is the town that was late in replying to official documentation, is it not?"

DeLarouge nodded. "It is, sire. I had long interviews with both men, who seemed to believe the entire town had been possessed by demons. I sent men from the neighboring town of Blenacre to investigate, and they have confirmed my fears." DeLarouge looked at his king, who shook his head slowly, as if he could change the news he was about to receive by force of will alone. DeLarouge continued, "According to the sergeant in charge, the entire town, including the military outpost, is in disarray, and the populace is screaming out for this drug, Forever. His report said there were corpses in the streets, and half the buildings have been rendered useless by fire."

Silence descended in the king's quarters for such a long time that DeLarouge wondered whether Garnandius would reply. The duke risked a glance toward him and barely kept himself from gasping. After knowing this man his entire life and working directly for him since the death of his own father, he never had seen him so angry. Garnandius clenched his fists until the knuckles were white, his nostrils were flared, and the muscles in the side of his jaw flexed in barely controlled rage.

"How many?" the king growled through gritted teeth.

DeLarouge swallowed. "Four hundred souls in the town, sire, and double that in fighting men."

DeLarouge's stomach fell as Garnandius' expression changed to one of anguish. "Dear gods! Twelve hundred! Tell me a cure has been found," he almost begged. DeLarouge could only shake his head. King Garnandius of Trathlain scrubbed his suddenly careworn face with one hand before leaning forward and staring deeply into the eyes of the duke, who felt the full force of his cold anger. "Send a secondary force, DeLarouge. Burn what remains of the town to the ground, and have everyone put to the sword: men, women, children, and all the soldiers. Make sure the garrison is fully manned and make preparations to get enough supplies through to them." DeLarouge stood and backed away from his king. "I want this Haguana brought to justice also," Garnandius added. "You convinced me it was a good idea to allow him to keep functioning for a while, but his time has run out." DeLarouge could only nod. "Make sure word of this is spread. Make sure each and every citizen and soldier living in the border towns understands what fate befalls those who deal with Lavashians."

Garnandius gestured for DeLarouge to leave. The duke had almost reached the door when the cold voice of his king called him back. He turned to face the usually smiling face of his longtime friend with apprehension.

"No more games with Lavash, DeLarouge," the king almost whispered. "I will tear that country apart, stone by diseased stone, until its few rivers run red with Lavashian blood, and when I get hold of the emperor…" The king paused. "…I will wring the life from him with my own hands."

CHAPTER 10

As soon as the words had left his lips, the three women squealed questions at him like piranhas stripping flesh from a carcass.

"How is he?" Jocinta asked.

"Has he been looking after himself?" Della asked

"Is he thinking of us?" Matra wanted to know.

"Did father send you to rescue us?"

The hope in Della's youthful face almost broke Gremlaw's heart. He could only shake his head sadly and let them know what little information he had. "I was sent to infiltrate the Durana Trading Company, as Fitlock was identified as the main distributor of a drug called Forever."

Jocinta's face screwed up in a moue of disgust. "My Fitlock never would be so base as to deal in drugs. Whoever you are, you are wrong in that!"

Through eyes bruised and cut, Gremlaw looked at her and gently said, "I wish I were wrong, but he's using his distribution network to transport Forever because he thinks it will keep you three safe." He tried to rise, but the screaming pain that shot through his battered body made it impossible.

Silent tears rolled down Jocinta's face as she understood the reason behind her husband's actions. "My poor Fitlock," she cried. "I wish I could see his face just once more."

She tried to help Gremlaw become more comfortable. He gingerly took hold of her hand in his battered fingers. "I need time to heal," he told her, "time to think too." The young man smiled at all three ladies. "Despite my outward appearance, I can be quite resourceful." He added, "Don't give up all hope just yet."

Haguana's wife nodded silently as she rose and put an arm around each of her daughters, guiding them away from the young man, who allowed his eyes to droop closed once more.

*   *   *

Until now, Sergeant Thruxton had spent his life in the Trathlainian army in a border garrison that protected his kingdom from the empire of Lavash. No soldier had been more proud, and no officer's gear had been polished to a higher sheen for the king's visit four years ago. The sergeant could still recall the wonder and awe he had felt as the king had nodded to him personally. He had saluted his king as the summer sun beat down on all their heads. For a king to come all the way out here and personally acknowledge their part in the security of the kingdom? Thruxton could hardly believe it. He had been full of ideals when he had joined up so many years ago, ignoring the barbs and negative comments of fellows who saw this as a chore. If they longed for adventure in far-off lands, let them become travelers; Thruxton would make sure they had a kingdom to return to when they became sick and tired of foreign lands.

It was with a sense of trepidation and tempered pride that Thruxton had marched into Captain Harakas' office immediately after his summons. The captain had been reading something from a scroll as he entered, and Thruxton had snapped to attention before the man, staring at a fixed point above his captain's head.

A minute had passed before Harakas had looked up. "At ease, Sergeant." His tone of command rang out in the small, cold room he used as an office. "Take a seat." Thruxton lowered himself awkwardly into a wooden chair and sat with his back as straight as a spear shaft. Harakas took a breath and paused to consider his words carefully. "I've been reviewing your record, Sergeant, and I find it shows a soldier dedicated to the defense of this great kingdom. A soldier whose ideals and morals match those of the border defense Watch and furthermore a soldier who can be trusted to carry out the harshest of necessary duties to the letter."

Thruxton's chest swelled with pride as he listened to this speech. Finally, his years of faithful service had been recognized!

Now Thruxton was filthy—covered in sweat, blood, and the grime of smoke from the burning of Strathnave. He was tired and sick from the stench of death, decay, and fire. He had led his three hundred foot soldiers to the border town, barely believing the report Captain Harakas had given him. Yet he had seen the king's signature on the official order to decimate the little town and take over the garrison there, so it had to be true. Thruxton's long-held ideals had been smashed in one day of almost mindless slaughter. In this single day, he had abandoned his morals in order to kill the very citizens he had vowed to protect. The hollow in his chest was almost impossible to bear.

Worse than his own pain was the low morale of the men, both the small force with whom he had marched here and the few men who had been ordered here previously to confirm the report that Strathnave had been compromised. These men, soldiers all, were here for many reasons. Some had joined up for the thrill and glory, others for the king's wage; still more were running from difficult home situations. One thing linked them all; they had not signed up to murder Trathlainian men, women, and children in cold blood. Thruxton knew he needed to give these men a rousing speech for them to carry out their next abhorrent duty, taking the garrison. Even at the best of times, Thruxton had no particular oratory skills and never had been particularly loved by his men. Now his filthy, tired, demoralized soldiers had gathered outside the garrison buildings. No one had been sent inside so far, so Thruxton had no idea what they might find.

Wearily he stomped up a few stone steps and turned his dirt-streaked face toward his men. "Brothers!" he cried as loudly as his smoke-clogged throat would allow. "You all volunteered for this mission, yet none of us really believed our own men could be subverted in this way." Thruxton threw out one arm toward the squat stone fortress. "Now we'll find what we were told to be true!" Thruxton shouted now, anger fueling his words. "This town has been taken over by filthy Lavashians who have poisoned our brothers and used their underhanded tactics to rob them of their minds."

As if on cue, an officer sporting the red and purple of Trathlain royalty stumbled through the fort's gate, which hung open and un-guarded. Thruxton knew every man was watching this unfold, just as he was. The man's uniform was ragged and torn; vomit stained the roy-al purple of his tunic; and urine had soaked the front of his leggings. The pieces of armor he had retained were rusty and broken, and his weapons were missing. His complexion was nearly white except for the scabbed areas on his neck where it appeared he had scratched off his flesh. His vacant eyes shook in their sockets as he staggered down the stone steps toward Thruxton on unsteady legs. Each man could plainly see his mouth working as he gibbered something unintelligible while he walked. Pasty faced and wide-eyed with madness, the unnamed of-ficer finally arrived next to Thruxton, who gagged at the rotten stench rising from him.

"Help me," the soldier begged, drool falling from his slack lips. "I need Forever!" The poor soul sobbed uncontrollably as he fell to his knees. "Forever!" he howled.

Sergeant Thruxton drew his sword slowly while looking grimly into the eyes of each of his men. "Motherless Lavashian bastards have done this!" He gestured to the blubbering unfortunate on the ground before him. Thruxton drew back his arm and stabbed it downward, through the neck of the officer who knelt before him, severing his spinal cord and ending his misery. He cleaned his blade on the man's cloak before gently removing the kingdom tabard. Then he saluted the fallen man and turned back to his men once more.

"Soldiers!" he bellowed. "I would expect the same treatment from each and every man here if I were to end up in the same condition as this brave soldier!" Thruxton allowed his point to sink in before calling for them to attack. The slaughter of fighting men began.

*　*　*

A week passed as Jocinta and her daughters nursed Gremlaw back to some semblance of health, and the three women became more at ease and friendly toward the youth. Gremlaw spent much of the time trying to devise some kind of plan to escape or at least be responsible for his own future in some way. He spent long hours sitting with his face pressed to the small, barred, square hole through which warm, stale air passed. Jocinta wondered what he was doing for all this time and finally asked one day after he had climbed back down.

"Seeing if I can keep track of our hosts," Gremlaw answered. "Sniffing the air too."

Jocinta considered this for a moment. "What have you learned?" she asked, genuinely interested.

Gremlaw sauntered silently over and pressed his ear against the door for a few seconds before gathering Jocinta, Della, and Matra at the farthest point away from it. Whispering urgently, he told them, "When the wind blows in from the east, I can smell the stables, so if you get any chance to run, head that way first. There's obviously some kind of water source near here, probably in the center of the buildings, and very few men are actually guarding the place. They have supplies sent in twice a week. These are brought by two different men each time, and they leave the same day. Of the five pieces of filth who dragged me here, the two smaller ones escorted one of Zha-Quin's lackeys away somewhere three days ago, so as far as I can tell, there are only about four people guarding us here."

"What does all this mean?" Matra asked. She had been more subdued than the other two, barely speaking until now.

Gremlaw decided there was little point in trying to sugarcoat their situation. "Four of us, four of them," he said, as the eyes of the two sisters widened in understanding. "I can be pretty fast when I need to be, and you three have the advantage of desperation."

Matra held her hands up to stop him from talking. "You expect us to fight men?" she hissed at him. "We are well-educated young ladies from a decent background and cannot be expected to fight trained soldiers."

Gremlaw looked at the three, his gaze falling on Jocinta before he spoke again. "I tell you this as the best kind of friend I can be to you and Fitlock. The net is closing in." He looked at each of them in turn. "Fitlock is in dire trouble for doing what he has for you. Now these Lavashians might wait to see if he can be of any more use, or they might have him killed." Matra and Della gasped. "Either way, the king cannot allow him to carry on committing what amounts to treason and will, at the very best, have him arrested or, at the worst, executed for his crimes." Gremlaw continued to speak despite their protests. "If any of these things happen to Fitlock, what use is there in keeping you three alive? They will kill you as if you're nothing more than cattle." Gremlaw could not meet their eyes as he added, "You'll be lucky if they don't ravage you first." Della's eyes went wide, and she clamped one hand across her mouth as if to stop herself from screaming. They all fell silent for some time.

"Have you any ideas?" Jocinta asked him a while later. The older woman had managed to comfort her daughters a little, whispering promises of safety into their ears.

Gremlaw scratched at one cheek. The scraggly beard that had sprouted there was more than annoying. "All I can think of is for you three to run if you get the chance," he said. "If you can get to the horses, steal them and head south. Either way, head south, avoid anyone you see, and stay out of combat, but if you're forced to fight, go for the groin, eyes, or nose. Scratch, bite, and kick them in their privates as hard as you can. Fight dirty, ladies, or they'll kill you." Gremlaw again eyed each of them in turn and hoped they understood his meaning when he said, "It's better if two make it back than none." It was Jocinta's turn to turn pale as she thought of losing one of her children.

Before Gremlaw could say anything more, the single door to the room flew inward and smashed loudly against the wall, making the three women jump. Two Lavashians with their wide, round eyes entered the prison cell, led by the sneering face of Zha-Quin, whose eyes lit upon Gremlaw with a hungry glare, as if he wanted to beat him senseless.

"Leaving time!" Zha-Quin chimed happily, as if they were all about to go for a picnic. "Standing to be." The two Lavashians who had come in with Zha-Quin entered the room and started toward Gremlaw, who vaulted from the low pallet and slammed his body into Zha-Quin.

"Run!" Gremlaw screamed at the three Haguana women as Zha-Quin cannoned backward.

Surprisingly, all three women jumped into action, and Jocinta even threw herself at one of the soldiers, sending him sprawling across the dirty, stained bed.

Gremlaw chuckled as he heard Zha-Quin's head crack against the stonework outside the door; however, his breath exploded from him as one of the other Lavashian captors pummeled a fist into his stomach.

Zha-Quin called out to them in Lavashian, "Do him no harm! The emperor wants him alive and unharmed." He grinned nastily up at Gremlaw while rubbing the back of his head. "To begin with at least," he added, still unaware Gremlaw could understand his language. "Hunt down the Haguana bitches and slaughter them!" Zha-Quin ordered as he regained his feet.

Gremlaw's heart sank as he thought of the chances facing the trio of his kinswomen out in the Lavashian wilderness through which he had been dragged. While he had been a prisoner, he had kept his eyes open until they had closed due to unconsciousness. He had not seen much in the way of plant or animal life that could sustain them, not even a decent water source.

Zha-Quin kicked Gremlaw's legs from beneath him, bound his hands before him, and dragged him outside to be tied to the rear of a wagon, which was hitched to a disheveled-looking beast of burden Gremlaw could only identify as some kind of donkey. Gremlaw was still so weak from his torturous journey through Lavash that he could not begin to put up a fight. All the healing he had done in the past fortnight, combined with a lack of any decent food for weeks, had weakened him to the point of exhaustion, and he stumbled forward against the back of the wagon. Leaning there and trying to regain his breath, he could not even pull himself into the back of the poorly maintained cart.

The young man heard screams of terror from somewhere behind him and realized Jocinta, Matra, and Della must have been caught. He dropped his head between his arms and wept.

CHAPTER 11

Zha-Quin and the other two Lavashians returned sometime after the screams had ceased and Gremlaw's tears had dried. Oddly, he did not see the smug, confident expressions on their faces he had expected and wondered whether the Haguana women had put up a fight before dying. When he looked at the men's unusually proportioned faces and saw no scratches or injuries, his heart sank. One of the men took up the reins, while his companion climbed into the bed to be accompanied by Zha-Quin. The latter watched Gremlaw trot along as the wagon trundled up the road.

"The emperor will break him," Zha-Quin told his companion in Lavashian.

The other man nodded silently, and Zha-Quin fell silent also. There was no banter between these new high-caste Lavashians and Zha-Quin, as there had been during Gremlaw's previous journey through the countryside. Gremlaw sensed these new Lavashians had no particular love for Zha-Quin and shunned his company. Gremlaw knew they had obeyed him in killing the Haguana women, so he probably outranked them, yet neither man seemed to want to be associated with the vindictive little Lavashian, which made Gremlaw wonder why. Despair welled up inside him as he thought of the three Haguana women and their horrific fate.

As he walked toward his new, unknown destination, he did not see the large dust cloud that had been kicked up somewhere south of him.

It had been just past sunrise when Gremlaw was lashed to the wagon. Midday had come and gone, and the harsh sunlight beat down on his head as he trotted along behind the wagon. There was a difference this time, however, as he had been allowed sips of water as he requested them throughout the day and even was given a few mouthfuls of dried fruit as the three Lavashians broke for a brief lunch. At the end of the day, when Gremlaw's final reserves had been completely drained and he started to stumble, he was lifted up to ride in the back of the wagon as it descended the gentle slope of a valley. With the final rays of sunlight and lengthening shadows creeping around him, he turned to look down the hill toward their destination.

* * *

Jocinta, Matra, and Della rode as if chased by demons. Night had drawn in, and a clear, star-filled sky stretched overhead, leeching the warmth from the dry air as soon as the sun set. Jocinta's horse stumbled, and she almost fell, reining the animal in before it slipped out from beneath her. Her exhausted daughters brought their own mounts to a stop near hers. All three women and the four horses they had managed to steal were just about to drop due to exhaustion, and Jocinta decided they all needed to rest. They had been blessed by luck so far; three of the horses already had been saddled for a journey, and the fourth had been laden with supplies, including skins of water. Running as if their lives depended upon it, Jocinta and her daughters had darted from the cell and past Gremlaw, who was actually laughing, and into the courtyard beyond. It appeared the compound where they'd been held had been a farm at some point, as there were a number of barns and outbuildings. In the middle of all the buildings was a square wall that stood about hip height and a well, as Gremlaw had guessed. The stables had even been where the young man had said, and Jocinta had led her daughters toward them as fast as her weakened legs would allow. Inside she saw the horses, ready to ride, and searched for a weapon of any kind to use against the two men who were closing rapidly on them.

"Get on a horse," she had called to Matra and Della, as her eyes lit upon a pair of pitchforks pointing out of a stack of rotting straw.

"Mother, what are you doing?" Matra cried in shock as Jocinta grabbed at the first pitchfork.

"Matra, I love you dearly, but if you don't get on that damn horse, I swear I will kill you myself!" Jocinta shouted at the shocked face of her older daughter.

Matra turned and tried to put her foot in the stirrup of the nearest horse. Her mother let out a furious scream, a wordless ululation filled with the pain and rage she felt at their treatment over the past weeks. The sound shocked Matra, and she yelled with as much force as she could, setting Della to screaming too. Jocinta crossed to the open end of the low building and launched the twin-pronged fork toward the nearest of the Lavashian men as hard as she could. Adrenaline and fear fueled her throw, and the soldier had to dodge as the metal spikes narrowly missed his legs. Both men slowed their pace, as they now faced armed and desperate opponents rather than fleeing women. Jocinta made for the final horse that had been saddled and nearly leaped atop it. Matra and Della looked at each other with wide-eyed shock; where had their mother learned this behavior?

Jocinta grabbed the reins of her horse in one hand and the second pitchfork in the other, wielding it above her head as if she were a mounted warrior. Driving her feet into her horse's flanks, she rode headlong toward the two men who were trying to kill her daughters. She screamed again before swiping the second fork at the pair, who had bunched together, cowering before this insane woman who seemed intent on throwing her life away to end theirs. Jocinta turned her horse at the last possible second, narrowly avoiding the men, who scrambled backward, caught completely off guard by her attack. She wheeled her horse, turning to the south before turning herself in the saddle and launching her second fork at the men. Then she set off toward the Trathlainian border, following her daughters, who already had rode off.

The three women now huddled against the cold, trembling against one another as the horses puffed steam next to them.

"W-what do you think will happen to us?" Della asked.

Jocinta tried to speak as calmly as she could through her chattering teeth. "We'll get home to your father and take him away to somewhere safe," she managed.

Conversation trailed off, as the three women were too cold to speak. Jocinta had not dared to light a fire, even if they'd had the foresight to gather wood.

* * *

Gremlaw's breath caught as he gazed down upon the beauty of the city that lay before them and seemed to be their destination. Towering, pure-white minarets, with sapphire highlights and roofed in gold, thrust themselves into the sky. Even the buildings between the towers, which surely served prosaic purposes, looked to be palatial in their construction and decoration. Palandine, where Gremlaw came from, had been constructed around a gray stone fortress, and most of the city's stonework had followed suit, lending drabness to the city that never would be seen here. Gremlaw stared in awe at the sheer size of the place. The valley in which this city nestled must have been at least three miles across at its widest point, and buildings caressed the slopes of both sides of the valley. The south-facing hills were covered from one end to the other with farms, presumably producing enough to feed the vast population contained in the city, and a thin ribbon of river snaked through the bottom of the valley. Gremlaw's mind struggled to comprehend all the details, and he thought the view must be overwhelming in full sunlight.

One of the two taciturn Lavashians, who barely had spoken all day, turned to see Gremlaw's expression. "Surprise, Trathlain?" he wondered in his exceptionally bad accent.

Gremlaw could only nod dumbly. "What's this city called?" he finally managed to ask.

Even Zha-Quin laughed at this. "Stupid you!" the Lavashian who had first spoken said. "Emperor's palace only, this." He pointed down the hill.

Gremlaw shook his head and, believing this to be a mistake due to the language barrier, said, "No. No, the whole city?"

Zha-Quin leaned over and rapped one of his knuckles against Gremlaw's head. "Be to listening! Is *all* palace."

Gremlaw swore beneath his breath. "All this for one man?" he wondered in shocked amazement.

The three snorted. "Trathlainian king not have palace?"

Gremlaw grunted a small laugh. "Not that big!" he replied, adding. "Maybe your emperor is compensating for something."

The Lavashians laughed, although they did not seem to understand the insult. Zha-Quin told Gremlaw, "Emperor, family, family servants, personal guard, personal guard servants. Palace grow and grow for thousands years."

"Madness," Gremlaw stated before he remembered he was their prisoner.

"Quiet, Trathlain!" Zha-Quin snapped, waving his fist before the young man's eyes.

The small, rickety wagon carried on toward the vast sprawl of the emperor's palace as night drew in, bringing a cold that rolled down the gentle valley's slopes like waves. Eventually they entered the courtyard of a building, where a contingent of ten Lavashian men in highly polished armor and midnight-blue capes stood at attention.

Zha-Quin dropped to the cobbled floor and approached them. "Sir!" he said in Lavashian. He saluted the man at the head of the band. "I have brought the prisoner, as requested."

The officer at the head of the contingent allowed his eyes to flick briefly to the face of Zha-Quin. "Requested, Zha-Quin?" The man's voice was like ice cracking as he spoke. "His most great and holy emperor *orders* you. Present the Trathlainian!" he snapped. To Gremlaw's immense gratification, Zha-Quin almost cowered before the man.

The Lavashian who had been in charge of Gremlaw since his capture in Strathnave ordered him to be untied from the wagon and dragged him roughly before the company. The officer assessed Gremlaw's condition and asked Zha-Quin, "Why does he appear to be beaten and exhausted?"

"He has been stubborn and attempted escape several times," Zha-Quin lied. "The language barrier has been a problem also," he added, still not realizing Gremlaw understood Lavashian perfectly.

The officer turned his hard face toward Gremlaw and spoke to him in his own language. "This man said you tried to escaping." His accent was a great improvement over that of Zha-Quin and his lackeys. "Is this a truth?"

Keeping his expression neutral, Gremlaw answered, "Zha-Quin and the men in his service have been abusive and kept me tied during the entire journey here." His nearly perfect Lavashian had the effect he'd assumed it would, as Zha-Quin's face drained of all color. "I had no opportunity to escape." Gremlaw allowed his voice to drop as he added, "I think he has developed unnatural feelings for me. That might account for his harsh treatment of me."

Zha-Quin gaped like an idiot as Gremlaw continued, embellishing the facts at his disposal in order to try to wreak some kind of havoc against the vile Zha-Quin.

"There were also a woman and her two daughters, one of whom was merely a child." Gremlaw shook his head in dismay. "It is only due to their care that I now live, and he had them killed before we came here." Here Gremlaw did not have to embellish his sadness. "According to Jocinta, Matra, and Della, Zha-Quin was violently intimate with all of them"—Gremlaw stared hard into the widening eyes of Zha-Quin as he added—"on a number of occasions."

"Filthy Trathlainian!" Zha-Quin almost screamed. Waving his arms wildly and threatening to pull out his sword, Zha-Quin approached

Gremlaw, who cowered close to this new band of men. "You never admit-
ted to having knowledge of Lavashian!"

The blue-cloaked and silver-armored commanding officer made an
almost offhand gesture. Suddenly Zha-Quin found himself facing the
unwavering points of three razor-sharp swords. The lamplight in the
courtyard flickered from the polished faces of the blades, glinting in
the huge eyes of Zha-Quin, which were now wide with fear as the commander stated, "Do not approach my prisoner, poisoner, or you will pay
dearly for it." His tone of disdain was evident, and Gremlaw began to
understand some of what might be happening here.

Before he could begin to think things through, however, he could
not resist one final dig at Zha-Quin. "Zha-Quin? During all the time you
spent dragging me behind your horse, you never asked me if I knew how
to speak your language."

Zha-Quin spluttered while the commander of the Lavashian troops
shook his head in disbelief. "Take the Trathlainian, and have him
cleaned for presentation to the emperor!" he barked. "Arrest Zha-Quin.
We will present him to the emperor also. Let the Light of Heaven decide
his fate."

Educated in obedience, the soldiers guided Gremlaw toward one
of the buildings that surrounded the courtyard, as Zha-Quin's weapons were roughly taken from him and metal shackles were attached to
his wrists. Even though Gremlaw had concluded he never would escape
Lavash alive, he was glad to see Zha-Quin taken by his own people. He
threw a nasty grin toward the vindictive little man who was escorted
away.

Gremlaw was taken into a small room with wooden seating along
one wall and shelving along its opposite. The floor was flagstone save
for a square in the center that was filled with smooth rounded stones of
varying sizes. One of his escorts showed him how to easily raise a bucket
to suspend it above the square. He was issued orders to wash, and his
clothing was taken from him, presumably to be burned, as it was next
to useless. After taking a soft-bristled brush from one of the shelves,

Gremlaw upended the bucket above him. This emptied into another device that sent the water down like rain. At first, he smiled at the feeling until his body registered the intense cold. He heard the men outside laughing as he gasped and shrieked.

After dousing in painfully cold water followed by a vigorous scrubbing, Gremlaw was deemed clean enough to be given a rough towel and some clothing common to Lavash. He dressed himself in the silky wraparound clothes, completing his ensemble with a pair of shoes as comfortable as any he had ever managed to steal. He was led into another area, bounded on all sides by buildings constructed from the sandstone common to the region, and held by four guards who applied a pair of shackles to his wrists.

Standing in silence, Gremlaw waited for whatever was about to happen next. His previous attempts to speak to the men of the squadron had been studiously ignored, so he turned his mind to the commanding officer's attitude toward Zha-Quin. It was obvious, to Gremlaw, that the officer had no respect for the low-minded Lavashian. He also had referred to him as "poisoner," which led Gremlaw to believe it had been Zha-Quin's responsibility, if not his plan, to use Forever within the kingdom. If this was true and Gremlaw had managed to thwart the plan, it would explain Zha-Quin's overwhelming hatred toward him.

Only the stretch of a few heartbeats passed before the rest of the squad formed up around Gremlaw, dragging Zha-Quin along with them. The vicious Lavashian had been stripped to the waist, and Gremlaw was surprised at how muscular he was underneath the heavy cloak he always wore. Tattoos crawled across various areas of his body; mirror images on either side of his spine and up to his shoulders had been inked into his flesh in curls and swirls. Gremlaw wondered how much pain he must have subjected himself to in order to gain these designs and what they might mean. Zha-Quin's expression had transformed from his usual look of smug superiority to one of trepidation.

"Did the Trathlainian give you any problems?" the commander asked one of the men who had been responsible for cleaning Gremlaw.

"None, my lord Vin-Sol."

Vin-Sol nodded. "Move out!" he barked.

The group journeyed through the vastness of the emperor's palace, which was seemingly endless, as the moon rose slowly into the sky, casting a pale glow that altered the shadows around the small group and in deep hiding places. Even though this was called a palace, Gremlaw saw all the features of a fully functioning city. Areas had been segregated from one another, however, meaning housing areas contained nothing but homes and shops were grouped together in neat rows in other areas. Public gathering spaces tended to be few and far between, little used and subdued in nature. As the predominant material for construction at this level was the light-brown sandstone Gremlaw had seen throughout Lavash, citizens had hung ribbons and strips of brightly colored cloth to relieve the monotony.

Marching along the center of a broad roadway, the company was given a wide berth, presumably out of respect, and Gremlaw began to understand the source of Zha-Quin's apprehension. Men, women, and the first Lavashian children he had seen, outside of Mishu's memories, lined up along the route they followed. What began as whispers and general gestures eventually transformed into shouts and cries of outrage, combined with jabs of accusatory fingers as they hurled abuse at the tattooed Lavashian. Zha-Quin hung his head as if ashamed, and Gremlaw felt a stab of overwhelming satisfaction. This man who had killed the three innocent Haguana women was hated more by his own race than Gremlaw himself seemed to be. Vin-Sol turned to see Gremlaw's triumphant expression before the young man had time to disguise it, and Gremlaw could have sworn he saw the beginnings of a smile at the corners of Vin-Sol's mouth. Gremlaw raised a questioning eyebrow, and Vin-Sol crossed over to him. The men of his squad changed position to allow their commander in, as if it were a natural function, like the drawing of breath.

"I know my reasons for hating him," Gremlaw called over the noise of the crowd, "but what's everyone else's problem?"

Vin-Sol's stoic expression did not change as he answered, "Zha-Quin belongs to a group of what we refer to as Lost Ancestors." Noticing Gremlaw's puzzled expression, he explained, "Years into Lavashian history, numerous groups with different leaders vied for dominance over the land. Eventually the strongest declared himself the first emperor of Lavash and settled here in this valley, where the whole palace has grown. Although most of the other groups eventually saw the sense in joining with the emperor in his new empire, some did not and continued their existence in far-off corners of the country. These rogue groups have been responsible for hundreds of attacks on pure Lavashian citizens over the years. Zha-Quin's tattoos mark him as an outsider. I was quite shocked myself to see them so prominently displayed over so much of his body." Vin-Sol frowned, an odd expression to see combined with his huge eyes. "Especially as he has been alone with the emperor in the past."

Gremlaw wondered why military action had not been taken against this Lost Ancestor tribe, but he did not have the opportunity to ask, as Vin-Sol moved back to his original place at the head of the company.

As if the group had crossed an invisible line, the construction of the buildings had changed from the sandstone blocks to what appeared to be gold-veined marble. Every surface Gremlaw saw was so highly polished it was as if they were walking through a hall of mirrors. Gremlaw caught sight of a skinny, hollow-eyed man with a scraggly beard and harrowed expression on his sunken face. Fear and shock almost made Gremlaw jump when it finally sunk in; this was his *own* reflection. Zha-Quin had starved and abused him to such an extent that he looked like one of the desolate victims of Forever he had seen in Strathnave. His heart sank as he realized he never would see his mother or Huleta again, never set foot on Trathlainian soil again, and he was surprised how much he missed his home. He was being marched toward one of the cruelest and most ruthless people in the known world—a man who had sanctioned the use of poisonous narcotics in order to gain a foothold in the kingdom. He knew his chances of leaving this palace, let alone the country, were slimmer than a blade of grass. He would die in this country, far from the only home he ever had known.

A whirlwind of emotions washed through the young man's consciousness as they slowly passed increasingly opulent buildings. At approximately the same moment as his first step faltered, commander Vin-Sol ordered a halt. Gremlaw was escorted into a building built completely of marble, the red veins running through it ominously blood red to his eyes. He sank into a pile of cushions and was almost instantly asleep when one of the soldiers who had escorted him shook his shoulder. In his state of near exhaustion, Gremlaw barely could register what was happening; something was thrust into his hands, and it took a few moments for him to realize it was a plate of fruit—not the dried fruit or the beans he'd previously had but brightly colored, fresh, succulent fruits.

Tears welled at the corners of his eyes as he picked up a small, oval, bright-green fruit and popped it into his mouth. Sweet nectar-like liquid exploded in his mouth as he mashed the thing with his loose teeth. The flavor was so intense and his palate so denied any other flavor for so long that it was almost painful to Gremlaw at first. Tingles ran down the sides of his tongue and into the depths of his throat as the deprived nerve endings finally awoke to taste again. He crammed as many of the ovoids into his mouth as he could, relishing the juice that dripped down his chin. He bit into a large, pale ball with fuzzy skin over the juicy pulp. He was surprised to find a pitted, oval piece of wood in the center until he recalled plums from Trathlain having something similar inside. Gremlaw gorged himself until his deprived stomach threatened to rebel.

One of the soldiers noticed and squatted beside him. "Go slowly," he advised. "That half-breed filth used you badly." Gremlaw shied away from the man, as if he were about to steal his food. "True warriors of Lavash," the soldier continued, "either treat prisoners with kindness or execute them cleanly. This is yet another sign the Lost Ancestors should be exterminated. They give all of Lavash a bad name." He gently patted Gremlaw's shoulder as he rose and turned away.

Gremlaw finished his fruit and was passed a cup of wine, which he drained in a few gulps. He suddenly felt uncomfortably full and immensely drowsy. Reclining on the cushions, he drifted into a deep sleep almost immediately.

The rocking woke Gremlaw seemingly years later. His eyes fluttered open to see the blue sky above him and the outlines of brilliant white buildings pass him by. Two men carried him in a makeshift stretcher— long poles with a strip of material between them. Once the guards realized he had woken, he was set to his feet and took a few moments to stretch his muscles, amazed at the recuperative powers of fruit, wine, and sleep. He felt more alert than he had in days, and most of his pain had receded to a dull ache as they continued their odd journey.

If Gremlaw was stunned by the exterior of the imperial palace, he felt as if he had shrunk into insignificance at the sheer size and luxury of the inside of the buildings. They finally had arrived in the buildings occupied by the emperor himself. Everywhere he looked, he saw examples of opulence and splendor unlike anything he had ever dreamed. The palace of Trathlain looked like a rundown brothel in comparison. Silks hung everywhere; every piece of metalwork Gremlaw saw was pure gold, silver, or both. Marble statues, fully clothed in traditional dress and painted to increase their resemblance to those after whom they were modeled, stood regally atop massive blocks of intricately carved stone with inscriptions he could not see properly. Gardens full of exotic-looking flowers and elegant fountains cast their reflected colors into the corridors and passageways through which Gremlaw was marched. He had been split from Zha-Quin, and now he and five soldiers, including Vin-Sol, made their way toward the emperor.

Upon arriving at a vast pair of gilded doors, they halted as Vin-Sol spoke to the guards outside. They in turn spoke to someone inside, and a few minutes later, one of the massive doors opened. Gremlaw found himself in a long hall with open windows all the way along one side, offering a view over the city-like palace. Vases of flowers and plants filled the air with their mingled scents as Gremlaw quickly looked around. At the far end of the hall, wide steps led up to a raised dais upon which sat a vast chair, padded with thick cushions. Groups of men and a few women stood on the steps, all wearing different outfits of different design but the same dark crimson. Taking in their features, Gremlaw realized most of them were blood relations and surmised their position on the stairs was relative to their position in line to the throne.

Vin-Sol and his men prostrated themselves, facedown on the floor, before their emperor as he sat impassively upon his throne, staring into Gremlaw's eyes as if he were able to read his mind. Emperor Haz-Tchin-Kavash had a reputation for being merciless and driven in his goals, which included the invasion of Lavash, so Gremlaw was surprised to find himself facing an old man. Despite the heat, which could not be dispelled by a wind blowing in through the open windows, the frail emperor was wrapped in layers of clothing, leaving his small head poking out in an almost comical fashion. Wisps of hair jutted up from the translucent skin that was stretched taut across his skull. Gremlaw could make out the zigzagged blue-and-red lines of blood vessels running through his skin and noticed the lower lids of his massive eyes sagged so low that the raw, red flesh beneath easily could be seen. The emperor's stare bored into Gremlaw's orbs as if red-hot knives were being driven into them.

Wondering what the etiquette might be regarding his particular situation, Gremlaw inclined his head slightly while maintaining eye contact. If he was going to die, he thought, he would do so with dignity rather than fawning to this man.

"Rise, Commander." The emperor's voice was deep and powerful despite his thin frame, and Gremlaw began to reconsider his initial impression. "Report," he ordered. Vin-Sol spoke at length regarding all he had learned since meeting Gremlaw, including the allegations of abuse concerning Fitlock Haguana's family. Kavash made a dismissive gesture with his hand, and the squadron and its commander filed out immediately, leaving Gremlaw and the Kavash family alone.

"So, Gremlaw," Kavash said in almost accent-less Trathlainian, "how is my old friend Wattiern DeLarouge?"

Gremlaw had been expecting the emperor to have some kind of intelligence regarding his situation that could be used to elicit answers from him. "I haven't seen the old boy for quite a while," he replied flippantly in perfect Lavashian, which produced no reaction from the emperor.

The old man pulled a stick-thin arm from within the layers of cloth covering his body. Pointing at Gremlaw, the sagging flesh of his arm swinging, he roared, "You have been identified as a spy, an enemy to the great empire of Lavash. You have hindered some of my plans involving the kingdom of Trathlain and ruined any future use I might have made of the Durana Trading Company. What have you to say?"

Gremlaw thought momentarily before raising his shackled wrists slowly toward Emperor Haz-Tchin-Kavash and asking, "Diplomatic immunity?"

CHAPTER 12

The almost incessant hammering on the wooden planks, which was his main door, finally roused Fitlock Haguana from his drunken sleep. He cast his blurred vision around the once neat, well-appointed sitting room where he previously had entertained the minor nobility who lived nearby. Empty bottles littered the room, and most of the furniture had been pushed aside; a few of the wooden chairs had even been overturned. The hearth had not been swept for days, the embers of the last fire going cold long ago as he had laid off all his household staff, endowing each with a generous sum to tide them over. Once the house had been his alone, Haguana had gotten to the serious business of drinking himself to death.

"Curse that meddling little thief!" Haguana said to no one as he searched for a bottle to ease the pounding inside his head. News had spread like wildfire concerning the crown's response to the situation in Strathnave, and Haguana had come to the realization he never would see his beloved wife and daughters again. Even if they somehow had managed to escape their Lavashian captors, his fate was sealed. He expected to be caught and hanged before long, now that the king's forces were involved. *Still,* Haguana thought, *if I stay drunk, I probably won't even realize it when my neck snaps at the end of the hangman's noose.*

Haguana was so disoriented he could not tell whether the hammering sound came from the rear of his house or from within his own head. He managed to find a quarter-full bottle of some clear-brown liquid and pulled the stopper, releasing the pungent fumes. The first few swallows came as a painful surprise; liquid fire drained down his esophagus and pooled in his stomach, which threatened to rebel. Haguana had spent the better part of two days pouring alcoholic drinks into himself without bothering to eat anything; in light of this, it was easy for him to become quite drunk within only a few minutes of sucking the spirit from the bottle.

Haguana stood on swaying legs and gesticulated at the door with his final bottle. "Come and get me then, you filthy Lavashian scum!" he screamed before downing another huge gulp of spirit. He looked at what remained in the bottle then launched it across the room to smash against the door. A single lantern, now burning low, sat on the table where he had shared family meals, and Haguana punched at it wildly, missing it the first time but eventually sending it flying toward the doorway.

He heard a loud whump as the vapor from the liquor was ignited by the lamp. Flames licked up the wood of the door and ate at the tinder-dry papers that had been strewn around the floor, taking hold of the building's structure with sickening speed.

The muffled screams from outside barely registered as Haguana watched the fire tear through his ruined home. He fell back into the chair he had slept in as the fire began to suck all the oxygen from the air. Finding it difficult to breathe, Haguana's body tried to save itself without his consent, and a reflexive shock sent him over backward, chair and all. Tears dripped down his face as his oxygen-deprived, alcohol-addled brain convinced him he could hear little Della screaming for him.

"Soon," he sobbed as the flames began to roar around him, "soon, my love."

"Fitlock!" Jocinta Haguana screamed as she saw the drunken form of her husband half obscured by a large padded chair.

"Jocinta?" Haguana slowly twisted his head around to try to see if his wife actually had returned to him. Hope exploded in his chest as he caught sight of the woman he had known and loved since childhood. "Jocinta, is it really you?" Through the smoke and haze, Haguana could just make out a thin figure crawling toward him. The pall of depression he had allowed himself to sink into broke open like a cracking egg, and he summoned enough strength to clumsily kick the chair away from his body, clawing his way away from the intense heat of the fire toward this newcomer. He reached for the woman's outstretched hand, relishing the feel of another person's hand in his own. This woman was real!

"Jocinta!" Haguana cried, as his eyes finally focused enough to recognize her face. "It is you!"

"Fitlock, we have to get out of here!"

Haguana nodded, and the pair desperately made their way from the fire and toward the rear of the house.

Matra and Della clung to each other as the only home they ever had known burned with their parents inside. A few people had gathered to watch the flames envelop the roof and belch smoke high into the air. Forbidding them to follow her, their mother had left them at the rear of the property and disappeared inside the burning home. The two sisters clung to each other, sobbing as glowing embers—remnants of their home—gently floated down around them. From the front of the building came a hissing sound, as some of the townspeople had formed a chain and were vainly attempting to douse the flames with buckets of water. As Matra and Della watched with tears cutting tracks in the grime and soot that covered their faces, the main timbers in the roof of their home gave way and collapsed into the upper story. In turn, the fire-weakened joists that formerly supported the upper floor gave way, raining burning wood and fire-blackened stone onto the ground floor. The sisters screamed as their lifelong home collapsed on top of their parents, who had not yet reappeared.

* * *

Emperor Haz-Tchin-Kavash laughed a deep, hearty laugh at Gremlaw's audacious request. The standing members of the imperial family alternated between chuckling and gasps of shock.

"You have an unusual sense of humor for someone in your unique situation," Emperor Kavash finally said. "Unfortunately there is no provision for a Trathlainian embassy, so I must decline your request." Gremlaw allowed his shackled wrists to fall back down as the emperor continued. "I have at my disposal a woman who has become an expert in the art of drawing secrets from the minds of anyone with whom she has contact. I am reliably assured it is an invasive process, shatteringly painful, and ultimately damaging to the mind of the victim." Gremlaw tried to swallow the lump of fear that formed in his throat as the emperor said this in an almost conversational tone. Kavash clicked his fingers once, which summoned two fully armed guards, one to either side of Gremlaw. "I will not pretend I have regrets in taking this decision. You forfeited your life as soon as you entered my empire, and I will know all your secrets." He looked deeply into Gremlaw's eyes. "If you even have any," he added. He made a dismissive gesture with one hand, and the two guards dragged Gremlaw away.

Fifteen minutes later, Gremlaw had been securely chained to a thick wooden table in a dimly lit room. His arms and legs were immobile, and he could see nothing, save for the unadorned walls and ceiling of the cell. He had been left here to await whatever fate this woman was about to inflict on him, and bitterness spread through his psyche. What would happen to his mother now that he had failed in the task set by DeLarouge? What of Huleta? Surely, they would be cared for considering the lengths to which he had actually gone. Wouldn't they?

Bitterness grew inside the young man, forced to serve his country then given no help or backup whatsoever. Footsteps, light and quick, disturbed his thoughts, and he had to fight the urge to call out to whoever approached. A hooded figure appeared in the semidarkness and stood silently at his side, like some dark figure bringing death. *This*, Gremlaw thought, *must be the woman who will invade my mind.*

* * *

Matra and Della had sunk to the ground hours ago. A caring neighbor had wrapped a knitted shawl around their shoulders in a vain attempt to fend off the creeping chill that had seeped in with the morning high tide. The girls sat side by side, their dirty heads leaning against each other as they stared vacantly into the smoking ruins of their home, now their parents' grave. Neighbors continued to pour water on the ruins, cooling the embers so the ruins could be searched for the bodies of Jocinta and Fitlock Haguana, while keeping an eye out for anything that might benefit the two devastated girls.

Matra drew in a deep breath. "It's just you and me now, Della," she whispered. Matra felt her younger sister nod gently even though she did not speak. "I'll take care of you, you know?" Della nodded again and tightened her arms around her sister's thin frame. The rhythmic stomping of marching feet roused both sisters from the despair they found themselves in, and they rose to meet the local watchmen who had marched up to them. Matra and Della looked as far as possible from the well-bred young ladies they actually were. Both girls wore torn, ragged dresses, the material hanging from their skinny bodies like rags on scarecrows. Each girl's normally silken hair was matted, twisted by the wind, and full of evidence of the landscapes through which they had journeyed in the recent past. A layer of grime had been left on both Haguana girls, from the dusty plains of Lavash as well as the sooty smoke from the fire at their home.

"I am deeply sorry for your loss," the young watch captain said in a deeply respectful tone. "And I beg your forgiveness in this present matter," he continued. Matra thought he had kind eyes as he said, "We have reason to believe your father, Fitlock Haguana, lived in this house." Matra and Della nodded. "Neighbors say he was inside this house when it burned. Can you confirm this to be the case?"

Matra nodded as Della broke into fresh tears once more. "Our mother went in to try to save him," Matra said. "She did not come out either."

The watch captain nodded sadly and spoke once more. "You both have my sympathies." His tone was so low that he could not have been overheard by the rest of the watch soldiers who stood by. "If there's anything I can do to help in your time of need, merely ask." He paused for a while, allowing his gaze to flick between the stares of both girls. Neither one asked for anything. He pursed his lips. "Well, then," the captain said, "I shall take my leave, ladies." Turning on one heel, he barked a few orders at the men who were pointedly avoiding looking at the two sisters and began to walk away.

"Captain!" Matra called after him. "What did you really want here?" she asked in a raised voice.

The captain halted and stared at the ground before slowly turning back and replying, "I have orders from King Garnandius to arrest one Fitlock Haguana for the crime of treason."

"Ah." This simple sound was the only indication Matra gave that she had heard him.

Moments later he turned and marched his small force of men away.

Matra and Della stood by the four Lavashian horses they had stolen to make their escape and waited. Neither sister knew what they were waiting for, yet in the absence of any other kind of plan, this is what they did. Della stood with her back against the horse, which almost had died to get her here, as she stared at the ruined stones that formed the base of her former home. Some trick of the light, or more tears, must be responsible, Della thought, for it appeared as if a section of the pavement at the rear of the house was moving. Putting the experience down to stress, Della turned to her sister, who was gaping at the slice of pavement. Della looked back to see a hand emerge from a subterranean realm and feel around the edges of the slab it had raised.

* * *

Vainly Gremlaw thrashed his head from side to side in an attempt to dislodge the woman's fingers from his head. Desperation built inside him as her icy fingers traced his temples. As cold as a corpse's fingers, her grip tightened on his head. A small cry escaped his lips as he felt her presence invade his mind. This was not the gentle probing Mishu had attempted; this was an outright violation. Issuing from the woman's ice-cold flesh, the worm of her mind burrowed in through his skull and lunged deeper into his conscious mind, like a stiletto being driven through his brain.

Gremlaw thrashed, inside his own mind now, as he fought to dislodge the agony of the overpoweringly strong mind of this woman invading his own. As he asserted his will, she increased the pressure and insistence of her presence. His back arched off the surface of the table, limbs straining against the chains that held him as knives of searing-hot pain shot through his brain. *This is it*, Gremlaw managed to think through the agony. *This is how my life will end.* Chained to a table, in a foreign land, never able to see his mother or Huleta again, his mind systematically being ripped apart from within.

Gremlaw's thoughts were steered by his invader and turned to DeLarouge and his team of misfits, Dron and Mishu. As soon as he thought of the renegade Lavashian magician, the woman gripping his head plundered each and every memory he had of her. Gremlaw felt her personality withdraw slightly, as if puzzled by these memories. Gremlaw's mind was directed to recall the memories that had been transferred to his brain, and like a snake striking, his inquisitor was among them, plundering and rifling though those recollections.

Searing agony shot forth within Gremlaw's mind—a violent thrust of raw, burning energy he could not begin to control. It seemed as if screaming waves of agony issued from every section of his body—from the iron-hard muscles, which were in a constant state of rigid spasm, to his skull, which felt as if it were being forced apart from within. White bliss suddenly coated Gremlaw's conscious mind as his assailant was thrown clear across the small room to smash against the wall and slide slowly to the floor, her head slumping forward inside her hood.

Gremlaw's body, covered in a sheen of sweat, relaxed against the cool wood of the table as soon as she had been expelled from his mind. He lay panting, the pain from his wrists and ankles now making itself known. *More pain*, Gremlaw thought bitterly. *Just what I need.* Eventually he opened his eyes and looked around for the woman who had collapsed, finally spotting a pile of brown material wedged in the corner of the room. Still chained to the table, Gremlaw had no way of doing anything but call to see how she was.

"Are you dead?" he croaked.

He received nothing in response but a rustling of material. A few seconds passed as the woman slowly dragged herself to her feet, leaning heavily on the table for assistance. With trembling hands, the Lavashian woman reached up and pulled back the cowl that previously had hidden her features. Gremlaw was struck by her beauty; her raven hair and pale skin contrasted with her enormous amber eyes, which seemed even larger to him than the others he had seen. What struck him most, however, was the abject sorrow and pain that radiated from those eyes. They were red rimmed, and tears had tracked their way down her face.

"How do you know that woman?" she asked in perfect Trathlainian.

"What?" Gremlaw squeaked in puzzlement. She reached for him again, and he nearly screamed, desperately recoiling until he understood she was releasing his wrists.

"The Lavashian woman who molded her mind with yours, Mi-Zhu-Quan. How do you know her?"

Knowing there was little point in lying, as this woman probably could just rip the truth from his head, Gremlaw told her, "Mishu is married to a man named Dron. They were both responsible for what little training I had before I was forced into this trip." Even after all of Gremlaw's abuses, his natural flippancy returned. "Why do you ask?"

She glanced into his eyes as if reading his very soul before releasing the chains about his ankles. "I ask because the woman you know as Mishu"—she turned those huge lupine eyes upon Gremlaw again, almost making him flinch—"is my mother."

CHAPTER 13

Four scrawny, hard-ridden, sad-looking horses plodded along the trail that led through the grasslands to the east of Silverdane. Bright moonlight helped the beasts pick their way along the path as they carried their four weary travelers away from the port. Dropping down a small incline, the rider at the front swayed uneasily in his saddle and dismounted at the bottom of the hill to look around. There was a copse of trees here with a patch of evergreens growing along one side, providing shelter from the cool wind that followed them down the hill. The loamy soil was soft, with a comfortable layer of dry-leaf mold covering it, and there was plenty of dry firewood for a small fire. One of the riders pulled things from a saddlebag and laid out a large bowl filled with water for the horses. Another tied bags of feed up for the animals to regain some of their strength, while another grabbed a handful of dry leaves and grass to roughly brush their coats down.

Once a small fire had been lit, and the horses tended to, the four riders huddled between the evergreens and fire, trying to keep warm. The smallest of the four looked up at the tallest and smiled. This acted as a catalyst, and all four members of the Haguana family found themselves grinning as if they were moon touched.

"Do you think your hair will grow back?" Della asked her father.

Fitlock shrugged one shoulder and said, "It doesn't matter to me. Everything I hold dear is within my reach." He gently stroked Della's dirt-and-tear-streaked cheek to demonstrate.

"I still can't believe you managed to escape into that vault," Matra said. "I said it was a stupid idea when you had that added to the cellar. I'm glad you did now, though. Just how did both of you manage to fit into such a small space?" she wondered.

Jocinta cleared her throat and replied, "It took a great deal of squeezing and pressing against each other." Then she laughed.

"Mother!" Matra exclaimed in shock.

"What do you mean?" Della inquired. "I don't understand." Her cross expression made the other three chuckle, and eventually she joined in too.

"I didn't realize," Fitlock said, "the charlatan who installed it left a hidden access for him to rob me blind!"

"Yes, we really ought to think of some way to thank him for that," Jocinta added, and the family all laughed again.

"What will we do now, Father?" Della asked.

"Go far from here and begin new lives," Fitlock said. "You'll have to forget who you once were and adopt a completely new identity."

Della's face became thoughtful in the firelight. "Then I shall be a princess," she declared triumphantly. She looked at the astounded faces of the other three and began to laugh again.

Suddenly the mood turned somber as Matra said, "I wonder what happened to Gremlaw."

Fitlock shook his head; he still found it difficult to believe the man who had scared the wits out of him by dropping silently onto his desk had ended up in the same place where his family had been held. He had been astounded at the tale related, in fits and starts, by his family as they had ridden from the ruins of their home under the cover of darkness. He owed a great debt to the skinny thief, and it was a debt he would be joyful to repay. "He's quite a resourceful young fellow," he told his family. "I'm sure he's fine."

* * *

"My name is Mar-Tshi-Srin," the Lavashian woman said. "I was told my mother was executed for crimes of treason against the empire." She added in her soft voice, "I'm ashamed to admit I believed all I was told." She hung her head as Gremlaw lowered himself to the floor. The young man stumbled due to the pain radiating from his ankles, and she reached out a hand to help him.

Gremlaw recoiled from her corpse-like touch as if she were poisonous. "I'm fine," he stated flatly.

Mar-Tshi-Srin's hand dropped like a stone. "I apologize," she said sadly. "I promise I'll never meld with your mind again." Her face fell. "I regret I've been lied to and used for the evil purposes of others."

She wore such a dejected look that Gremlaw felt a stab of pity and gritted his teeth as he reached out his hand. He was pleasantly surprised; her hand was as warm as his as she took it, intertwining her fingers with his. He relaxed as he realized the icy chill he felt before must have been due to the magic. He smiled at Mar-Tshi-Srin and asked, "What's next?"

The small Lavashian magic user shook her head. "I need a little time to think." She looked into his eyes again. "Not here, though. Someone might come along. We need to get to my apartments." Dragging him along with surprising strength, Mar-Tshi-Srin made her way through corridors and doorways, up short flights of stairs, and around the perimeter of decorated gardens until she led him to a suite of rooms she said were hers.

Gremlaw looked about as he lowered himself onto a padded couch upholstered in vermilion silk and complete with luxurious cushions. Although small for a room in this building, the space was easily five times the size Gremlaw had lived in growing up. Heavy drapes flapped in the warm breeze that gusted in through the open windows, revealing a small garden beyond. Expensive-looking works of art garnished the marble walls as lifelike statues regarded Gremlaw with their dead-eyed stares.

Mar-Tshi-Srin paced back and forth along the longest line she could find, tapping the fingers of her right hand against her jaw as she walked. Gremlaw shuddered involuntarily as he recalled the cold, jellied sensation of those same fingers on his skin.

"The emperor must pay for what he has done to me!" she declared to Gremlaw. "Ripping me from the arms of my mother and convincing me she was dead. Making me extract information from people, making me *hurt* people, and telling me he had my best interests at heart!" Mar-Tshi-Srin was almost shouting now, and Gremlaw worried that someone might overhear. "When all this time he used me for his own sick purposes!" She rounded on Gremlaw and pointed a finger at him, which made him recoil again. "I will see him dead!" she spat through clenched teeth.

Gremlaw sighed and blew out a breath. "Can't we just go?" he asked forlornly. "I just want to go home." He was aware he sounded almost childish, but he did not care. "Please?" he begged.

Mar-Tshi-Srin's eyes softened for a moment as she regarded the battered, bruised, half-starved young man she saw before her. "I would like to," she said in a small voice. "I want to meet my mother, but I can't allow the emperor's crimes against my family and me to go unpunished."

Gremlaw's heart sank lower than it had before. To have this newfound freedom taken from him as quickly as it had been given was a fate crueler than he deserved. Hate and rage started to form within his chest, but he was so tired that a numbing sense of apathy took over instead.

Mar-Tshi-Srin noticed the volatile emotions coursing through him and offered him her bed and some food. "We should be safe until nightfall in a few hours," she told him. "Try to get some rest. I promise I'll do everything I can to get you home safely."

Gremlaw gorged himself on exotic fruits again before slumping onto the bed Mar-Tshi-Srin had indicated. Closing his eyes, he inhaled deeply; the bedding held a vestige of her scent, and he drifted off to sleep almost immediately.

Soon, however, a hand was shaking his shoulder, and he groaned, "What now?"

"It's nighttime," Mar-Tshi-Srin stated. "Time for a private audience with his imperial majesty, the Light of Heaven." The few hours Gremlaw had slept had not dulled the Lavashian woman's intensity. "These belong to my manservant. He won't miss them." She handed a bundle of clothes to Gremlaw, including a pair of supple boots. "Will you need assistance dressing?" she asked. Gremlaw gave her a long stare, and she turned away, shrugging.

Gremlaw wrapped himself in the voluminous clothing, which consisted of a long cloak-like garment with sleeves and a deep hood, which he drew over himself to hide his features. The boots felt as if they had been made for his feet, even though the rest of the clothes were enormous on his small frame.

"Follow me and remain quiet. Do not speak to anyone unless they address you specifically," Mar-Tshi-Srin instructed as she handed him a three-foot katana-like sword in a scabbard. "Conceal this beneath your robe, and show it to no one," she cautioned. "You're supposed to be my acolyte and therefore should be ignored."

Gremlaw did as told as the brown-robed Lavashian woman led him through the labyrinthine palace toward what he was hoping was some kind of exit. Soon, however, he realized he was being taken into the heart of the palace, directly toward the emperor.

The pair arrived at huge gilded doors flanked by two tall guards holding evil-looking halberds with two-foot-long curved blades. Mar-Tshi-Srin stood before the two men who looked down at her. "I will see the emperor," she said in a commanding tone.

"The Light of Heaven is not to be disturbed," one of the men replied gruffly.

Rather than argue with them, the diminutive woman simply pointed toward them. Both men crashed to the floor, unconscious. Gremlaw tightened his grip on the handle of the katana as Mar-Tshi-Srin casually opened the expansive door and slipped inside. Gremlaw noticed a similar pair of men collapsed inside the room and wondered how much power this young woman had. Once again, the opulence with which the imperial apartments were decorated took Gremlaw's breath away, as priceless examples of crystal ware vied for space alongside gold castings encrusted with precious gemstones. Gremlaw followed Mar-Tshi-Srin through several rooms adjoining one another before discovering Emperor Kavash. The old man sat in a conspicuously Trathlainian chair and was oblivious to their presence as he wrote something at a desk.

"I left orders not to be disturbed!" he snapped, noticing Mar-Tshi-Srin as she approached.

"I have information regarding the Trathlainian spy," she told him in a submissive tone.

Emperor Kavash's eyes flicked to Gremlaw's hooded form for a second, and he demanded, "Who is this?"

"My acolyte," Mar-Tshi-Srin answered smoothly. "I allowed him to end the spy."

The emperor allowed a brief look of surprise onto his face before speaking again. "Approach then, and speak of what you know."

Mar-Tshi-Srin's small form took two steps toward the man who was systematically trying to overthrow the kingdom of Trathlain and, before he could react, grabbed his head on both sides.

Emperor Haz-Tchin-Kavash's body went rigid, as if struck by lightning; his spine locked into a line that continued down his legs and even pointed his toes. His hands alternated between tightly clenched fists, and rigidly pointed fingers. Gremlaw actually saw the color as it drained from his face, saw his tongue work back and forth inside his wide-open mouth like a worm struggling out of the earth, and thought his eyes might pop from his head as they bulged with the pain of whatever Mar-Tshi-Srin was doing to him.

"You lied to me!" she spat at him through teeth clenched in rage. "All my life you told me my mother betrayed you, and now I've found out the truth." The emperor body had gone into a complete state of shock, and tremors rocked the length of his aged form. "*You* are the one who betrayed us both!" Mar-Tshi-Srin shouted into the old man's constricting face. Kavash's tongue flapped against his lips, and his eyes rolled into his skull as a deep scowl dragged his thin eyebrows down.

Gremlaw's gorge rose as he recalled how it had felt to have lived through a similar experience. He watched in horror as the most powerful man in the known world urinated in his clothing. As the scent of feces assaulted his nostrils, Gremlaw noticed someone walking toward them from a different direction than the one from which they had entered.

"Apologies, Uncle..." the newcomer's voice announced. This new, younger version of the emperor had entered the room. Gremlaw watched as the man gaped at what was happening to the emperor and saw that he was about to open his mouth to scream for help. Although Gremlaw had been through many ordeals in recent weeks, he managed to dart toward the man, drawing the katana and laying the diamond-sharp edge against his throat.

Mar-Tshi-Srin spat upon the vacant face of the emperor before releasing his ancient skull by pushing it roughly from her. She turned to Kavash's nephew and dropped to one knee. "Greetings, Light of Heaven," she said, falling forward and placing her forehead against the cold marble of the floor. Gremlaw continued to stare at the man as he examined his uncle's drooling, excrement-stained body, the breath from which still whistled audibly in the room. Mar-Tshi-Srin either had decided against killing Kavash or had been interrupted before she could. Gremlaw glanced at the ancient emperor and wondered what had been left of his personality.

Silence reverberated in the room for untold lifetimes until the new emperor of Lavash came to his senses. His eyes fell on the depths of Gremlaw's hooded face, and he pushed the end of the blade from his neck before he spoke in a deep, commanding voice. "For personal service to myself," he said, "you are both granted release from Lavash." Gremlaw's hopes rose as the message set in. "Know, however, once a full week has passed, you'll both be considered traitors of the empire of Lavash and ordered to be executed on sight." The new emperor turned and made his way to the desk where his uncle continued to drool over his fine silk clothes.

Mar-Tshi-Srin led Gremlaw from the imperial apartments and back toward her own. "I wish to take a few personal things with me," she explained to the dumbfounded young man as she breezed through the palace.

"What…what just happened?" Gremlaw asked, as the pair reached her suite.

Mar-Tshi-Srin looked confused. "In what way?"

Gremlaw could only gape. "In the way you marched into the emperor's private rooms and changed him into a mindless wreck!" he cried. "And how come the other one just let us go?" he added in complete confusion.

Mar-Tshi-Srin smiled. "Politics here can become quite violent. Lavash's new emperor has had to fight for his life on numerous occasions." She was digging through her possessions, apparently looking for something important. "Secretly he wants to steer the empire in a different direction, one based on peace and trade rather than force and underhanded dealings. Ha! Found it," she said, secreting something inside her robe. "I think Lavash is on the verge of a new era." She looked into Gremlaw's eyes and added a little nervously, "Shall we go to Trathlain?"

EPILOGUE

Mar-Tshi-Srin was beside herself as the carriage she had ordered clattered through the cobbled streets of the Trathlainian capital. She glanced at Gremlaw, who sat opposite her, smiling as he watched her nervousness increase with every step the horses took.

"She will love you, you know," the young man reassured her for the hundredth time. Their journey from Lavash had been a period of ease for Gremlaw. It turned out Mar-Tshi-Srin was quite wealthy, and she had paid for all their travel arrangements—from carriages to ships, to all the board and lodgings in the inns and hostels they had used—and had outfitted Gremlaw with a new set of clothing after having his hair cut and beard shaved off.

The pair had become good friends during the journey. Their long hours spent in travel had been filled with Gremlaw speaking about the memories Mishu had left inside his head.

"It's really weird," he had told the girl, who had insisted he call her Marshi. "You and I are about the same age, but I remember the nurse handing you to me when you were born." Marshi had smiled at his confused expression. "I also remember it nearly driving me mad when they took you from me." Gremlaw had swallowed so as not to cry, and Marshi had patted his hand.

"Tell me about this Dron fellow my mother married," she had said, changing the subject.

Gremlaw felt nerves of his own as the carriage pulled into DeLarouge's palace, although not as deep as the near fright Marshi was going through. She looked up at the imposing gray fortress that was DeLarouge's ducal palace and shuddered. "Does my mother really live here?"

Gremlaw laughed and shook his head. "Not quite. Her home is a little more colorful than this." They exited the carriage, and Gremlaw led Marshi through the hedge and up to the multicolored tent where her mother and Dron lived. Afternoon sunlight filtered down, reflecting varicolored light from the multitude of dyed cloth.

Gremlaw laid a finger on his lips and called out in imitation of a common porter, "Delivery for Dron!"

A few moments later, the enormous man stood in the small antechamber staring openmouthed at Gremlaw. A massive grin crossed his brutish face, and he almost shouted Gremlaw's name before the young man could quiet him with gestures.

"Come outside," Gremlaw whispered to Dron. "Is Mishu home?" The bulky man followed Gremlaw out to where Marshi stood, wringing her hands. Dron's eyes fell upon her hooded figure, and he raised his eyebrows to Gremlaw, who quietly explained, "It's a long story, and I will tell it, but this is your stepdaughter, Dron."

The large man paled as Marshi took down her hood, and he gazed upon her Lavashian features. "You look just like her," Dron rumbled quietly. He took hold of her trembling hand and squeezed it gently. "She believes you died a long time ago, you know?"

Marshi nodded as she glanced at Gremlaw. "He told me all about it. When can I meet my mother?" she asked nervously.

Dron gave her a gentle smile. "Right now. Come."

The three slipped off their shoes and entered the tent Dron and Mishu shared, Dron taking the lead as he guided them into the main living space. Mishu sat cross-legged on some cushions, a book spread before her as Dron approached. Without looking up from her reading she asked, "What was it, my love?"

A stupid grin was plastered across Dron's face as he stepped aside, revealing Marshi. "It was something for you," he said.

Mishu looked up, catching sight of the younger version of herself who stood before her and frowned. Rising smoothly, her book forgotten, Mishu stepped toward the woman who was her daughter with something like the fear one feels when approaching a deadly snake. The two women—one older, one younger, yet definitely related—faced each other. Barely breathing and with a visibly trembling hand of her own, Mishu reached for Marshi's face and tentatively stroked her cheek. Marshi's large eyes became wet with tears as the older Lavashian woman said in her native tongue, "You are my daughter, Mar-Tshi-Srin." Mishu's lips quivered as decades of pain washed away.

Spilling tears down her chest, Marshi nodded and replied in fluent Trathlainian, "You are my mother, Mi-Zhu-Quan." She smiled. "Mama." Mishu made a choking sound and grabbed Marshi in a hug that promised she never would let her go again.

Gremlaw grinned at Dron, who had tears in his own eyes. The big man gestured to the doorway, and the pair left the reunited Lavashian women alone.

"Something tells me they're going to be at that for a while," Dron observed after they had changed shoes and left the tent.

Gremlaw looked at the visibly shaken man and said, "For the rest of their lives hopefully."

Dron nodded. "Come with me," he ordered. "I've got something to show you." It was Gremlaw's turn to nod, and he followed the mass of humanity around the side of his tent. Dron led Gremlaw to a different section of the hedge that separated this section of DeLarouge's grounds and pointed along the barrier. "Keep to this hedge on your left, and keep going. You'll know what it is when you see it." Gremlaw made a face, as if wondering what Dron was up to, yet the monster like man simply curled one side of his mouth up and gave him a shove. "Go and see," he said. "You've earned it."

Gremlaw had not appreciated how vast the land on which DeLarouge's palace sat actually was, and it was a few minutes before he came to an archery range where a tall figure was pulling arrows from straw targets. Gremlaw approached the archer, who was dressed in leather trews and a long gray coat. He noticed the bright-blond hair that had escaped from beneath her hat. Gremlaw's stomach clenched, and his throat went dry as he realized who she was.

Huleta stiffened as she heard him approach and called behind her without turning. "I said I'd come back once I'd had a few hours' practice, Dron."

Gremlaw stood silently; his mouth worked, yet no sound issued as he gazed upon the woman he had loved since childhood, the woman he had convinced himself he never would see again.

Sensing something amiss, Huleta turned to see what the problem might be. She paused, and Gremlaw watched as a range of emotions played across her beautiful features, from confusion to absolute happiness. She ran to him, slamming her body into his and knocking them both to the ground. Her arms locked around Gremlaw possessively as if she claimed him as her own and professed she would never let him go. Gremlaw buried his nose in the crook of her neck and inhaled, closing his eyes as the overwhelming, heady scent of her filled him.

Dawns could have come and gone, worlds might have collided, and stars burned themselves out, but Gremlaw would not have cared. All that mattered in that instant was her scent: a warm mixture of blond hair, a flowery scent she had begun to wear, and just Huleta. Gremlaw's arms locked about her, and he pulled her to him as she sobbed into his ear, making small sounds that told of her loss and joy. When she eventually pulled her head back as if to check whether it was actually him, Gremlaw saw the face he adored, the face that had kept him going through all his trials in Trathlain and Lavash, and finally he knew he was home.

EPILOGUE

G ray clouds scudded overhead as the small gathering stood at the graveside, the final resting place of Gremlaw's mother, Cyrena. Gremlaw stood beneath the darkening skies, looking down into the hole in which his remaining parent had been placed. Situated in the royal cemetery—a tribute to the service Gremlaw had performed for the kingdom—and placed beneath an oak tree with a view across the city of Palandine, it was far from the pauper's grave he might have been able to afford. A priest from the local church had performed the service, ensuring Cyrena's spirit passed into the next world. The few people who had attended, who had been there for Gremlaw, paid their respects and slowly made their individual exits, leaving Gremlaw and Huleta standing by the hole.

Gremlaw recalled the events that had taken place after Huleta had finally managed to unwind her body from his in DeLarouge's garden. He had looked into her tear-reddened eyes and saw the relief and happiness she felt at his return transform into an expression of pained hopelessness. He remembered the feeling of his stomach plunging down into the depths of his guts, thinking she would reject him once more.

"Grem," she said in a thick voice, "you need to come with me." Huleta grabbed his hand, pulling him toward the large ducal palace of the DeLarouge family. Through the gap in the hedge and across a neatly tended lawn dotted with summer flowers and bordered by shrubs she led him. They approached the rear of the palace by way of a gravel path bordered on either side by short, evergreen hedges, climbed a set of aging stone steps spotted with orange lichen and green moss and entered the massive building through a rough wooden door.

Inside, the roughly plastered walls were an off-white color and the flag-stoned floor had a thin patina of dirt across its rough surface. Huleta dragged Gremlaw down the wide hallway, passing doors to rooms whose contents remained closed off from his eyes. Halfway along this hall, the blond woman halted before one of the doors; this, to Gremlaw's eyes, seemed no different from any of the others. Pausing to glance into his eyes with her own cornflower blue orbs, she squeezed his hand and opened the door.

The chamber was fairly small, possibly half the size of his childhood home and contained a bed; a pair of simple chairs; and a chest, atop of which was a jug, bowl, and cup. The walls were unadorned, as was the ceiling, while drab curtains wafted lazily in the breeze, which failed to clear the smell of death from the small room. Gremlaw's eyes registered these few details in a flash before settling on the form in the bed. Logically the young man knew it must be his mother, but the shrunken, withered face of the old lady lying close to death was as far removed from his last memory of her as it could be.

"DeLarouge did this?" he asked through clenched teeth.

"No, love," Huleta told him, warming his heart with her words, "he brought her here when the deterioration began a few weeks ago." Gremlaw seated himself next to the dying woman. He could not believe it was his mother, and he listened to her labored breathing, wheezing slowly in and out of her mouth. Her thin hair had been laid out in a fan on her pillow, the graying strands nowhere near the light brown he recalled. Her cheeks were sunken and lined, lips pale and slack, while her eyes moved beneath the lids as if she dreamed.

"But the poison...?" He trailed off. Huleta gripped his arm with her other hand.

"He never gave her any, It was a ploy to get you to work for him."

A lump formed in his throat as he came to understand his mother was finally about to die. Possibly, not right now, yet soon. The young man leaned forward and took her hand in his, almost flinching at the ice cold he felt in her fingers.

"Ma, can you hear me?" No response was forthcoming and tears welled in his eyes at the thought that he would not even be able to say goodbye to her. Huleta stroked his arm as her own tears came.

The two young people stayed at Cyrena's bedside for hours as her breathing slowed, eventually coming in short gasps that became further and further apart. Her chest rose, then fell, and never rose again. Gremlaw leaned over and kissed his mother's cheek.

"Finally at peace, Ma," he whispered. Huleta stood beside Gremlaw and took him into her arms, rocking him gently as he sobbed into her shoulder.

A gentle breeze moved the scudding clouds overhead as Gremlaw turned from his mother's grave to the woman he had loved since childhood. He took both her hands in his and looked deeply into her eyes.

"I don't want this to be a day remembered in sadness," he began, "and I know I haven't got much to offer besides my love,"—Huleta's eyes widened as Gremlaw dropped to one knee—"but will you do me the honor of becoming my wife?" Huleta's hands flew to her mouth in astonished surprise, tears of joy springing to her eyes,

"Oh, Gremlaw," she said in a choked voice, "of course I will! I love you."